Ella could feel her attention being drawn to Luke.

His presence seemed to fill the air around her, making him impossible to ignore.

His eyes scanned the water as he navigated the river. He appeared to be concentrating hard, but despite his solemn expression, there was no denying he had a very handsome face. His blue eyes were perfectly set above a straight, symmetrical nose, full lips and a strong jaw covered with light stubble. His hair was thick and dark and swept back from his forehead, which was creased in concentration. He looked fit and his limbs were long and tanned, muscular but lean.

Luke's gaze met hers, and flustered at having been caught, she turned back toward the front of the little boat. The breeze against her face provided welcome relief from the heat of the morning and she closed her eyes as she tried not to worry. She had no idea what would happen next, but for the moment, she and Liv were safe and that may be the best she could hope for.

T0014747

Dear Reader,

Despite spending forty summers on the River Murray in South Australia, I have never set a book in this part of the world. After the region was inundated with floodwater last summer, Ella's story took shape in my head, and now I have my first Riverland story.

Ella arrives in the riverside town of Pelican's Landing after escaping a traumatic relationship, only to be faced with more trauma when she is caught up in the flood event. After she and her four-year-old daughter are rescued from the swollen river by a gorgeous stranger (and his dog), she finds herself stranded in the country town.

Her planned onward journey is derailed by the flood, and as Ella waits for a way out, she is gradually enveloped by the town's residents—the local GP, community nurse, police officer and other parents— who make her feel welcome and encourage her to stay. But Ella is not convinced that Pelican's Landing can provide her with a safe haven. Can she find a forever home in this country community?

I'd love to hear from you if you've enjoyed this story or any of my others. You can visit my website, emily-forbesauthor.com, or drop me a line at emilyforbes@internode.on.net.

Emily

Rescued by the Australian GP

EMILY FORBES

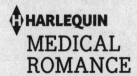

HARLEQUIN
MEDICAL
ROMANCE

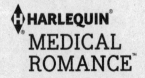

Recycling programs for this product may not exist in your area.

ISBN-13: 978-1-335-59537-9

Rescued by the Australian GP

Harlequin Enterprises ULC
22 Adelaide St. West, 41st Floor
Toronto, Ontario M5H 4E3, Canada
www.Harlequin.com

Printed in U.S.A.

Emily Forbes is an award-winning author of Medical Romance novels for Harlequin. She has written over thirty-five books and has twice been a finalist in the Australian Romantic Book of the Year Award, which she won in 2013 for her novel *Sydney Harbor Hospital: Bella's Wishlist*. You can get in touch with Emily at emilyforbes@internode.on.net, or visit her website at emily-forbesauthor.com.

Books by Emily Forbes

Harlequin Medical Romance

A Sydney Central Reunion

Ali and the Rebel Doc

Bondi Beach Medics

Rescuing the Paramedic's Heart
A Gift to Change His Life
The Perfect Mother for His Son
Marriage Reunion in the ER

London Hospital Midwives

Reunited by Their Secret Daughter

Rescued by the Single Dad
Taming Her Hollywood Playboy
The Army Doc's Secret Princess

Visit the Author Profile page
at Harlequin.com for more titles.

For Charlotte.

Thank you!

Having an editor who makes my job easier, my stories better, and who genuinely champions romance authors is a wonderful thing.

Thank you for your words of wisdom, your support and your enthusiasm. You are very much appreciated! This is one of those times when I can honestly say, "I couldn't do it without you."

Here's to the next book,

Emily

CHAPTER ONE

'HIGHER, MUMMY, HIGHER!'

Ella gave her daughter another push on the swing, sending her soaring through the air. Her little legs stuck out, brown and thin against the blue summer sky, as her blonde pigtails streamed behind her. She squealed and laughed, and her giggles were a balm to Ella's tired, tormented soul. She was exhausted, so tired that her head ached constantly and now her joints were starting to ache too.

She lifted her face to the sun. Despite the early hour, she could already feel the warmth in the air. It would be another hot day she knew as she felt the sun beat down on her. She was dressed in a long skirt and a long-sleeved shirt but, even though she couldn't see anyone else nearby, she resisted the urge to push up her sleeves. She hoped her outfit gave the impression she was being sun-smart but, in reality, her clothes hid a secret.

Her eyes followed the arc of Liv's body as she swung through the air but her thoughts drifted away. Ella had hoped to stop in Pelican's Landing for several days to give her time to catch her breath after the long drive. She'd been driving for days; she was tired and dusty.

She looked past the playground equipment and out to the river. She'd had visions of swimming in the river, of washing away the grime and dirt on her body and in her head, but the river was in flood and, in fact, she could barely even see it over the temporary levee bank that had been built to hold back the flood waters.

She'd driven halfway across the country, over three thousand kilometres across the desert from Western Australia, but in her haste had failed to notice that the eastern states were under water. The Darling and Murray Rivers were flooded and the water had swallowed everything in its path, houses and all, as it made its way from the outback and the mountains to the sea. She was tired and dusty but hadn't even been able to enjoy a swim. All water activities, including swimming, had been banned due to the flood event.

But she had stayed in Pelican's Landing anyway. She couldn't face driving any further. Not just yet. Over a week on the road with just a four-year-old for company hadn't been a lot of fun, and navigating the desert highway alongside massive road trains, grey nomads towing caravans and backpackers in their campervans, had added to the difficulty.

She'd stopped in Pelican's Landing because she liked being near water. She could breathe then. There were plenty of towns just like this one along the river but she'd liked the name. She loved watching the majestic birds glide through the air on the thermal currents, free and easy. All the river towns were in the same predicament—flooded, struggling. If she'd realised this before she'd left Western Australia, she might have headed north, but she really needed a break from driving. And from sleeping in her car.

She could afford to stop here for a few nights. The night skies were clear. The trees were magnificent. The birdlife varied. It was what she was used to. She wasn't a big-city person; she needed space. She felt safer when she had room to move. Room to run.

If the river hadn't been flooded and the town suffering because of it, she might even have considered staying longer. She might have looked for work—just something temporary. Something to top up her income and perhaps put some money in the bank to help her and Liv start over. Cleaning houseboats or cleaning the facilities in the caravan park would have been perfect—it would need to be something she could do with Liv in tow—but jobs were scarce because of the floods.

The town survived on the tourist trade, in particular the summer holiday period, but because of the flood, which was the biggest in fifty years, all water activities on the river had been banned. There was no swimming, no fishing, no boating, no houseboats, no skiing and, therefore, all holidaymakers had made other plans. They hadn't seen any point in coming for a holiday at the river if they couldn't use it. The town was suffering from the lack of overnight tourists and the few day trippers who visited weren't enough to make a difference.

The town had been divided by a massive levee bank. What she imagined would normally be a picturesque town, with its historic old buildings, marina and paddle steamers, had been split in two by it. It even blocked the view of the river from the main street. But at least the levee bank meant the caravan park could stay open. Even if there were no tourists there had been engineers, labourers and machine operators employed to build the bank and they had needed somewhere to stay. Most of them had moved on now but the caravan park remained open.

Now it was home to dozens of people who had been forced to move out of their riverfront houses because of the floods. Most of these people were retirees and, while Ella knew her daughter would have liked some playmates, she was happy with the lack of families in the park. She wasn't obliged to make small talk with other parents at the playground and that suited her. She preferred to keep her business to herself. And she didn't want Liv to form friendships just to be dragged away again.

They'd have to move soon. She needed to find a job and somewhere to settle before Liv started school. They were sleeping in a tent; that wasn't a viable long-term option but she couldn't afford to rent a cabin and a tent was better than sleeping in the car. The little bit of money she'd managed to save wasn't going to last much longer. She got a single mother's benefit every fortnight, but she was trying to save that, knowing she'd need a deposit in order to get a roof over her head.

Her plan was still to head north, to Queensland ultimately, somewhere with good weather and maybe the chance of a job and the opportunity to finish studying. Queensland had a booming tourist sector; she was sure she'd be able to find work doing something. She was smart, and pretty, and could make herself presentable if she had a little bit of time and money for some new clothes. Something decent from the thrift shop would do. She was thin—probably too thin—but at least that meant almost anything in a thrift shop would fit her and she knew she could make almost anything look okay.

'Push me, Mummy!'

Ella had drifted off into planning mode and Liv's swing was slowing down. 'Use your legs, Liv, you can keep yourself going,' she answered, needing to give her tired arms a rest. 'Five more minutes and we'll get an ice-cream,' she added, trying to sweeten the deal.

She checked the handbag that was strung across her body, hoping she had enough money for the treat. It was another three days until her next government cheque hit her bank account and that wasn't money that she could fritter away. But Liv deserved a treat. Ella had some tins of tuna and some pasta, and the caravan park manager had given her some eggs and fresh tomatoes. She should be able to stretch that out to make dinner for three nights, which left her just enough money in her purse for two ice-creams.

She pushed her hair out of her eyes as she zipped her bag closed. The wind had picked up and was stirring the surface of the river, forming little waves, capped with white. She looked

to the trees as a flock of sulphur-crested cockatoos took to the sky, screeching in protest. She
wondered what had startled them.

Movement to her left caught her eye and, as
she turned her head, she saw water trickling over
the levee bank. Ella frowned as she tried to process what she was seeing, initially thinking the
wind must be pushing the water over the bar-
rier. But then she watched in horror as the levee
bank began to collapse and a torrent of water
gushed into the caravan park as the bank gave
way. Within seconds, muddy water was swirl-
ing around her ankles as the river continued to
force its way through the levee. Tree branches
of all shapes and sizes swept through the breach,
rushing towards her. The water kept coming and
was up to her knees before she reacted.

She had to move. She and Liv needed to get
to higher ground. The water wasn't stopping and
the force as it flowed around her almost knocked
her off her feet. If they didn't move, they were
going to get swept away or, worse, sucked under.
If she lost sight of Liv, she knew she'd never find
her in the muddy water. Neither of them would
stand a chance against the current.

She pulled Liv off the swing, grabbing her
by one arm.

'Ow, Mummy, you're hurting me.'

There was no time to apologise. There was no time to think about the bruises she might leave on her daughter's skin. No time to worry about what anyone would think if they saw the marks. Ella looked around, frantically searching for higher ground, looking for somewhere safe to flee to before the water swallowed them.

The water frothed around them; eddies formed and brown foam swirled past. Ella felt something slice into her right leg and she staggered as pain pierced her right calf and her knee almost gave way. Liv screamed as Ella momentarily lost her balance. She barely managed to keep her feet and straightened up, only to find that the water was now up to her thighs. She was running out of time.

There was an old set of monkey bars near the swings. It was their only chance. She limped through the water as quickly as she could, the current pushing her in the direction of the monkey bars. Her leg complained with every step but she had to keep going. Stopping was not an option. Liv's weight made covering the short distance difficult but at least she was going with the flow of water. She knew she wouldn't stand a chance trying to fight against it but, even so, she was still worried about getting knocked off her feet. She reached out with her left hand and grabbed the ladder of the monkey bars, not daring to relax yet. She pushed Liv up and hoped the equipment was firmly concreted into the ground.

'Climb, Liv. Hurry. As fast as you can. You need to get to the top.'

She hoped that would be high enough. She had no way of knowing when the water would stop rising but she was out of time. She had no way of getting anywhere else. She fought the current as it tried to prise her from the ladder, holding on with two hands now. As soon as Liv was halfway up, she scrambled up the rungs of the ladder behind her daughter.

She curled her toes around the rungs as the water swirled around her legs, realising she'd lost her sandals somewhere along the way. Sharp pain stabbed her right calf with each step. Liv was perched on the monkey bars. Ella scooted along and wrapped her arm around Liv's slender body, holding onto her firmly. She couldn't lose her.

Her leg throbbed, her skirt was ripped and she could see a nasty gash in her calf. She made sure Liv was stable on the play equipment before tearing off a piece of her skirt, thinking as she did so that she had nothing else to wear, but she needed to bandage her leg. She wound dirty, wet fabric around her calf and worried it might make things worse. It might not stop the bleeding and might give her an infection to boot. But she had to try to stem the blood.

By the time she finished, her clothes were almost dry but despite the heat she was shivering. She was feeling light-headed. She wasn't sure if it was blood loss, shock, heat, dehydration or all of the above.

'What happened, Mummy?' Liv was looking around, bewildered.

'Remember how I told you the river was flooded, full of water and dangerous? It got more flooded and came over the bank.'

There was no point explaining to Liv about the burst levee. It didn't matter now. She'd warned Liv not to go near the levee bank, her daughter was afraid enough already. This event wouldn't have helped. It frightened Ella—she could only imagine how Liv felt. Ella could see fear and confusion in her daughter's eyes and she fought hard to keep her own expression neutral. She didn't want her expression to mirror Liv's. She didn't want to frighten her any more.

Ella looked around the park as the water continued to rise. She was beginning to worry that it would keep rising and swallow their precarious perch along with everything else. Her heart was racing in her chest. She had no idea what to do next.

'Ella? Are you okay?'

She looked up at the sound of a man's voice calling to her. The caravan park manager and his wife were on the veranda of their house. The house was at the entrance to the park, at the top of the small slope, but the water was lapping at the steps to their veranda. Below them camp sites and cabins stretched down the hill to the river's edge all the way to the levee bank which had been holding. Until now.

Ella had put her faith in that bank, in the engineers and labourers who had built it. It was just another example of people letting her down.

'Stay there. Someone will come for us,' Bill called out.

She didn't know where he thought they could go. His comment would have been funny if their situation wasn't so dire. She could see the other park residents, clinging to their balcony railings. The ones who had cabins closer to the river had clambered onto the outdoor furniture. Ella knew most of the current park tenants were retirees. She hoped they had all managed to scramble to safety. She knew most of these people had already been evacuated from their houses due to the flood. They would have expected to be safe here.

'I don't like it here…' Liv's voice wobbled.

Ella didn't care for the place much either at the moment. What she'd initially seen as a quiet, almost idyllic spot to stop and gather their breath had turned into a nightmare.

'We're safe now. Someone will come to rescue us.' She mentally crossed her fingers, hoping Bill was right.

A siren blasted and Ella jumped, almost losing her balance. The wind had died down, disappearing as quickly as it had blown in, and the siren was sharp and piercing in the still summer air.

'What's that noise?' Liv put her hands over her ears as Ella gripped her more firmly, terrified she'd lose hold of her over this treacherous water.

'That's to let people know we need help,' she replied, even though she had no idea. She assumed it was an emergency siren, activated to let the emergency responders know they were needed. She hoped that was what it was for, and not to alert people of another impending disaster.

The water appeared to have stopped rising. It was a foot or so below the rungs of the monkey bars and Ella hoped it wouldn't rise again. She and Liv couldn't get to anything higher. They were stranded until help arrived. The water was too deep to wade through and flowing too strongly to swim through. She could see whirl-pools forming randomly, even without Liv, Ella didn't think it would be safe to try.

The caravan park and the adjacent bowling club and pub were completely surrounded by a levee bank. On Ella's left was the river and to her right, behind the other levee bank that *had* held was the town's main road. The caravan park was now a massive lake as the newly flooded area levelled out with the river. Ella hoped the levee bank to her right continued to hold otherwise the town itself would also be flooded.

She looked over to where their tent had been pitched. The tent and all their belongings had dis-appeared. Her car was still where she had parked it but the water was halfway up the windows. Everything they had, everything she owned, was either gone or destroyed. She hadn't had much to begin with but now she'd lost it all. She and Liv literally had the clothes on their backs and her handbag. Her heart sank as she surveyed the scene. Hadn't they suffered enough? Life could be cruel. She didn't need this.

She stifled a cry. She couldn't let Liv see her upset. She had to be brave for her. She had to stay strong. But, right now, she didn't know where she would find that strength. She'd been tested before but she'd always worried that one day something would break her.

Was this the day?

No. She shook her head. She wasn't going to be beaten. She was a fighter. She could do this. She tried to count her blessings as she clung to the play equipment. She still had Liv and they were lucky to be alive.

Although it didn't always feel like that.

CHAPTER TWO

'Maisie!' Luke whistled to his dog and waited for her to leap onto the boat and settle herself on the bow before he opened the throttle on his dinghy and pulled away from the mooring. He kept his speed low and scanned the river, watching out for submerged objects—logs, outdoor furniture, barbecues. All manner of things had been washed down the river with the flood and he knew that, as these things took on water, they often sank just below the surface. Colliding with one could damage the propeller, or worse, put a hole in the bottom of his small boat.

He'd grown up on this river. He and his friends had spent hours swimming and fishing and, as they'd grown older, they'd spent their teenage days skiing and their nights sitting on the bank under the stars, drinking beer and kissing girls. He knew the river well and, while he'd seen it in flood, he'd never seen a flood like this before. The last major flood had been well before he was born.

He fought the current, travelling upstream towards the caravan park. He'd heard the emergency siren and had responded to the call for help, as had plenty of other locals who had access to a boat.

He steered his dinghy through the break in the levee bank, following a couple of other small boats. He scanned the park for victims. He could see a State Emergency Services volunteer helping an elderly woman who was clinging to her veranda. The river had stopped rising, and she wasn't in immediate danger any more, but her cabin was surrounded by water and the only way out was in a boat.

He saw Bill, the park manager, with his wife on their front deck and lifted a hand in greeting. Bill and his wife were safe enough for now but he could see Bill pointing towards the river. He could see his lips moving but his words were drowned out by the sound of many engines. Luke turned his head, looking behind his dinghy back towards the levee bank and saw two figures perched above the water. He turned the rudder on the outboard engine and headed in their direction. As he got closer he could see it was a young woman and younger girl, perched on what must be some play equipment. The woman had a tight grip on the child, who was pointing at Maisie.

'…Dog on the boat!'

The noise of his outboard motor drowned out the first few words but Luke caught the end of the young girl's sentence.

'Stay, Maisie,' Luke instructed his border collie, who was now standing at the front of the boat and barking excitedly as Luke approached them. Luke didn't want her jumping in the river and trying to round them up. His dog was a strong swimmer but Luke knew she'd be no match for the current.

'Careful, Liv, don't lose your balance,' he heard the woman caution the child.

Both of them were thin and blonde with large brown eyes. Even though there appeared to be several years' age difference between them, perhaps fifteen, the similarity was obvious and he assumed they were sisters. The young woman pushed her blonde hair back, revealing a heart-shaped face and flawless skin. Her hair might be a tangled mess but she was stunning and Luke felt himself do a double-take, while hoping she hadn't noticed.

'Hi, my name is Luke. Can I give you a hand to get down from there?' he asked as he cut the engine, finally remembering he was here to get the two of them to dry land.

The woman appraised him with her large brown eyes before looking around, as if searching for a better option.

'Here.' Luke held onto the play equipment with one hand to stabilise the boat and reached down to his feet with his other hand to pick up two life jackets. 'These are for you. It's safer to put the jackets on before we move you to the boat. This one is small,' he said as he passed the first one up. 'Can you get it on?'

The woman was looking at him again. 'I think so,' she replied. She slipped the jacket over the little girl's head but then looked a little flummoxed as to how to secure it.

'Put her arms through the straps and then you can clip it together at the front,' he instructed. 'And now yours,' he said as he passed her the second jacket.

He busied himself securing the boat to the climbing frame while she got her jacket on. He attached a rope from the stern of the dinghy to a rung of the monkey bars. It wasn't perfect—he would have preferred to have had two ropes— but it would stop the current from pushing him away and it would have to do.

'What are your names?' he asked once he'd

tied the dinghy up and the young woman had had time to fasten the straps on her life jacket.

'I'm Ella,' she replied. 'And this is Olivia.'

'Okay, Olivia, let's get you into the boat.' He'd start with the little one. He reached up and lifted her off the play equipment. She weighed next to nothing and he picked her up effortlessly and sat her on the bench seat running across the middle of the dinghy.

Once she was settled, he turned back to the to help the other woman. 'Can you put your feet either side of the seat?' He indicated the seat in the centre of the boat where Olivia sat. 'That will distribute your weight evenly and keep the boat stable,' he explained. She wasn't going to be heavy but her high centre of gravity while she transferred into the dinghy could be enough to unsettle the boat.

She was staring at him but didn't move.

'Take my hand.' He reached out towards her but, rather than reassuring her, it seemed he'd spooked her. She leant back, withdrawing herself, leaning away.

Her dark-brown eyes were hard to read. Was she nervous? Scared? Was she afraid of the water? Afraid of him?

'You need to get in the boat. Hold on to me.'

'Mummy, get in!'

Mummy? This young woman was a mother? Luke saw her eyes dart to Olivia: her daughter. Ella looked to be in her early twenties, and Olivia looked to be about five. He wasn't judging but he had made assumptions—something his profession should have taught him not to do.

She looked nervous, frightened and vulnerable. She was very thin, and perhaps her slight build combined with her vulnerability made her look younger than she really was. Not that it mattered to him—he just needed to get her into the boat.

'It's all right. You'll be okay; you need to come with me.' He spoke slowly and calmly; he didn't want to startle her or add to her wariness. He didn't want to risk an accident.

Ella hesitated. She was reluctant to reach for him, reluctant to touch him. She didn't like being touched, unless it was by Liv. And she definitely did not like being touched by strangers—men in particular. But she knew she needed his support; she needed to be steadied. She only had one good leg and she had to make it into an unstable vessel. A very small unstable vessel.

Ella was looking into his eyes, trying to summon the courage to reach for his hand, when Liv pleaded with her to get in. He was watching her, and she saw his expression change as Liv called her 'Mummy'. Ella recognised confusion in his expression and saw the judgement in his blue eyes before he seemed to gather his thoughts and put them aside. She knew he would have made the same initial assumption that most people did—that she and Liv were siblings, not mother and daughter.

He was still watching her, waiting. 'You'll be okay,' he repeated.

He might have judged her but he was still there, waiting to help her. He had a calmness about his manner and his eyes, which were a startling blue, looked kind. She had to go with him; what choice did she have?

As she reached for his hand, the sleeve of her shirt rose up, revealing her wrist and the bruises that encircled it. They were fading from purple to yellow but they were still visible. She quickly pulled her sleeve down, hoping he hadn't seen them.

Her heart hammered in her chest as his fingers gripped her hand. His grip was firm but not painful and she willed herself to relax. He had come to help them; he wasn't going to hurt her. But, even so, she kept her left hand wrapped around the bars of the climbing frame, not prepared to give herself over to him completely just yet. His hold was light but strong. He wasn't forcing her to move. She knew she could withdraw her hand at any time if she wanted to; he wasn't overpowering her, he was simply offering support.

His skin was warm and soft, which surprised her. She'd expected his hand to feel rough but his skin was surprisingly smooth. She relaxed slightly, preparing to accept his assistance. He couldn't hurt her—not here. She had to trust him.

She forced herself to look away from his face, focusing instead on the boat. She stretched out her left leg first, not trusting her right leg to hold her weight. She didn't want her leg to give way, upset the boat and tip them all into the river. She placed her left foot on the bottom of the boat. The metal was warm under her bare skin as she made sure she had her foot firmly planted. She tried to keep her weight on her left leg as she lowered herself into the boat but that proved impossible.

The boat wobbled and she let go of the bars as she redistributed her weight. She shifted her weight onto her right leg to counterbalance the movement of the boat and that action sent a bolt of pain through her right calf. She winced and took in a quick breath of air, fighting not to cry out. She felt herself lean more heavily on Luke's hand as she tried to take some weight off her leg.

'Are you all right?'

Her gaze flew to his and she nodded, her teeth gritted, fighting discomfort. She wasn't about to whinge; she was used to pain and she'd learned to battle through it in silence. She saw his eyes move from her face to her leg and she sat down quickly on the seat next to Liv, in a hurry to get off her feet and to hide her leg from his curious gaze.

Only then did he let go of her hand, leaving her feeling as if she'd been cast adrift. She lifted her right leg over the seat, away from Luke, getting it out of view. She pulled her skirt down as best she could, trying to hide her makeshift bandage, which she could feel was soaked with blood. Fortunately, the fabric was dark. Maybe he couldn't see the blood; maybe he hadn't noticed.

He turned away from her, pulling on the cord to fire up the engine on the outboard and, once he'd got it restarted, he untied the rope that he'd fastened to the monkey bars before pushing them off, opening the throttle and puttering towards the main street.

Ella held onto the straps of Liv's life jacket and tried to keep her gaze on the front of the boat as

Luke steered it out through the gap in the collapsed levee bank and down the river. She could feel her attention being drawn to Luke. His presence seemed to fill the air around her, making him impossible to ignore.

She sneaked a glance at him under the guise of checking the contents of her handbag. His eyes scanned the water as he navigated the river. He appeared to be concentrating hard but, despite his solemn expression, there was no denying he had a very handsome face. His blue eyes were perfectly set in his face above a straight, symmetrical nose, full lips and a strong jaw covered with light stubble. His hair was thick and dark and swept back from his forehead, which was creased in concentration. There were little wrinkles at the corners of his eyes and she guessed him to be around thirty years of age. He looked fit and his limbs were long and tanned, muscular but lean.

She watched his hands on the rudder as the boat chugged down the river. He looked like a workman, but his hands were smooth and his nails were filed and clean. They weren't the hands of a labourer or a famer, despite what his breed of dog might suggest. She recalled how it had felt to hold his hand and she wondered what he did when he wasn't rescuing people.

Luke's gaze met hers and, flustered at having been caught out, she turned back towards the front of the little boat. The breeze against her face provided welcome relief from the heat of the morning and she closed her eyes as she tried not to worry. She had no idea what would happen next, but for the moment she and Liv were safe, and that might be the best she could hope for.

She opened her eyes as she heard the engine cut out and the boat bumped to a stop. Luke had pulled up around the far side of the levee bank that ran along the main street. A crowd of people stood on top of the bank, waiting to help the stranded caravan park tenants onto dry land. A man wearing a fluorescent vest emblazoned with the words *Murray Bunyip* raised a camera to his face and started snapping pictures. Ella turned her face away from the press photographer. She did not want her picture taken.

Luke tossed a rope up to a stocky man with a deep tan and a bald head who caught it easily, while a younger man looped a second rope round the front of the boat to hold it steady.

'Hey, Luke, I should have known I'd find you here.' A third person, an older man with close-cropped grey hair and wearing a police uniform, greeted Luke. 'What happened to taking the day off?'

'This is a day off.' Luke was grinning broadly; all the seriousness of his earlier expression had disappeared and, as his features relaxed, Ella thought he looked even more handsome. 'Mucking about in a boat on the river is the best sort of day.'

'Rightio, then, and who do you have to off-load?'

'This is Ella and her daughter, Olivia.'

'All right, let's get you out of there, shall we?' the policeman said as he reached out and offered a hand to help them to shore. 'My name is Sam. I reckon you should go first, Olivia.'

Liv was on the side of the boat closest to the bank. Ella nodded at her daughter and waited for Liv to reach out and take Sam's hand before she forced herself to let go of the straps on Liv's life jacket. The water was dirty and flowing quickly. She didn't want to think about Liv slipping and falling. If she slid down the levee bank she could disappear into the river in an instant.

'Put one foot on the edge of the boat,' Sam instructed Liv as he took her hand. Liv did as she was told and, once one foot was on the edge of the boat, Sam didn't wait for her to step across onto the bank. He was sturdy and tall and he plucked her from the boat before putting her onto solid ground.

'Your turn, Ella.'

Ella could feel herself shaking. She stood up, temporarily forgetting about her sore leg until her calf exploded with pain, and she quickly took her weight off it.

'Can you call Penny and ask her to take a look at Ella's leg? She's hurt it,' Luke asked Sam as Ella regained her balance.

'I'm fine,' Ella replied.

Luke looked at her but said nothing. He simply looked back at Sam with an expression that said, *ignore her and listen to me.*

'It's nothing, just a scratch,' Ella said as she glared at Luke. Despite the fact that he'd rescued them, had got Liv and her safely to dry land, he wasn't a knight in shining armour. He was a good-looking guy in a slightly battered, not very shiny, aluminium dinghy but that didn't give him the right to interfere in her well-being. Ella sensed that Luke was used to getting his way—Sam certainly didn't seem to have taken offence with him issuing instructions—but he wasn't the boss of Ella. No one was. Not any more.

She took Sam's hand and stepped out of the dinghy with as much grace as she could muster, given her sore leg and her dishevelled state. She gritted her teeth and forced herself to distribute her weight equally on both legs, despite the searing discomfort. She wasn't going to give Luke the satisfaction of seeing her grimace or falter again.

Ella had expected Luke to argue with her. She was sure he would want the last word: that was usually how things went. But, once she was on the levee bank he simply raised one eyebrow, shrugged his broad shoulders and said, 'Suit yourself,' before he restarted the engine, pushed himself off the bank, turned the boat around and headed back in the direction of the caravan park.

She watched him go before belatedly remembering her manners. 'Thank you,' she called out, hoping he'd hear her over the whine of his outboard motor, the noise of the crowd gathered on the bank and the sounds of the river.

He raised one hand in reply but he didn't turn around, didn't look back, leaving Ella strangely disappointed. He'd unsettled her and she wasn't sure why. No, it wasn't him, she decided. She wasn't going to let a man, a stranger, unsettle her. She was on edge, but that was understandable, given the situation she found herself in.

'Penny is a nurse at the local medical clinic,' Sam said, interrupting Ella's thoughts. 'She'll be happy to take a look at your leg for you.'

Ella shook the disappointment from her mind and tried to formulate a reply.

'That water is filthy. There are dead animals, contents of septic tanks and who knows what else in that river at the moment,' Sam continued, before Ella had a chance to respond. 'A small scratch can easily become infected. You don't want that,' he stated, mistaking her silence for reticence and trying to convince her of the foolishness of ignoring Luke's advice.

Ella looked around. She was bewildered, suddenly overwhelmed by the situation. She had no idea what she was supposed to do next. Where were she and Liv supposed to go? They had nowhere. Nothing.

She decided the easiest course of action was to follow Sam's instructions. That would save her having to make any decisions for herself right now and would hopefully buy her time to make sense of what had just happened.

'Sit down here while I make a phone call,' he said, settling them on a pile of sandbags and wrapping a silver insulating blanket around them both before pulling out his phone. Within minutes a woman in her late fifties pulled up at the side of the road and hopped out of her car. Sam waved her over to where Ella and Liv waited and introduced her.

Penny was no-nonsense, efficient but kind. She bundled them into her car before Ella even had time to thank Sam. She drove them up the main street, keeping a steady stream of conversation going as they passed the supermarket, a pub, a bakery and a few other assorted shops on the way up the hill to the high end of town.

'Is it just your leg that needs to be looked at? No other injuries?'

Ella shook her head.

'What about Olivia?'

'She's fine.' Ella felt bad that her answers seemed abrupt but she was fatigued and uncomfortable and close to tears. She was fighting hard just to keep herself together and didn't have the head space to make polite conversation.

Penny turned into the car park at the front of a modern building that appeared to house the medical clinic and an allied health facility. She ignored the parking spaces and pulled up directly in front of the main door. Ella slid out of her seat, wincing in pain, but determined to help Liv. Penny took one look at Ella's face and wisely didn't offer to help her get inside.

'The clinic isn't open?' Ella asked as Penny unlocked the door.

'No, it's closed on weekends. There's an after-hours number for emergencies or a hospital in the next town.'

Penny switched on lights and opened a door to a treatment room. 'Have a seat on the bed, Ella. Put your feet up,' she instructed. 'Olivia, why don't you sit here while I take a look at your mum's leg?' she said as she pulled a chair away from a desk.

'How much is this consultation going to cost?' Ella asked. She'd given up her objections now, too physically and emotionally exhausted to continue to argue, and it was probably wise to get the wound looked at. She couldn't afford to be sick but could she afford to pay for treatment? 'I have a health-care card,' she added. She hated being a welfare recipient but she'd learnt a long time ago to swallow her pride when it came to these sorts of benefits. There was no way she could afford health care without government assistance.

'Let's just see what needs to be done first,' Penny replied. 'I can't imagine there will be any charge above the government fee.'

Which meant there would be no out-of-pocket expense for Ella. 'Thank you.'

As Penny washed her hands and pulled on a pair of latex gloves, Ella pulled her ripped skirt up above her knees and tucked it around her legs. She needed to expose her injury but she didn't want Penny to see more of her legs than she needed to.

'Just lift your leg up for me,' Penny instructed as she stood at the edge of the bed, waiting to slide a waterproof sheet under Ella's legs. As Ella lifted her leg, her skirt rode up, exposing her upper leg. She saw Penny's eyes dart to the bruise that stretched along the length of her thigh. The bruise began at her buttock but she knew her skirt hid most of it and Penny was only getting a glimpse. It was turning yellow, it was obviously old, and Ella held her breath as she wondered if Penny would ask about it.

'That looks painful,' Penny commented.

'It wasn't too bad,' she lied. It had been painful—she'd fallen heavily, landing on her right hip. 'I bruise easily,' she lied again. That lie slipped off her tongue—she'd said it plenty of times.

Penny was watching her but Ella averted her eyes, looking at Liv as an excuse to break eye contact, but then wondered if she shouldn't have done that. Did it look as if she was warning Liv not to say anything? She'd become so paranoid. She had to remember that this move was a chance to start fresh, to reinvent herself and her life. And it didn't matter what people thought of her in Pelican's Landing, she wasn't planning on being here for long.

Penny turned her attention to the cut on Ella's leg and let the topic rest. Her makeshift bandage was soaked with blood. It hadn't been able to completely stem the flow of blood and was thoroughly saturated but at least that meant it peeled off easily. The wound ran from the outside of her shin, just below her knee, sloping down and back towards the top of her calf. It looked to be about four or five inches long and Ella could see it gaping at the bottom end.

She couldn't watch—it made her feel a little queasy—but thankfully she had an empty stomach and knew she wouldn't be sick.

'You'll need stitches in that,' Penny said as she cleaned the wound. 'I'll call Dr Donato.'

'What about those butterfly things? Won't that hold it?' Ella didn't want treatment. She didn't want more help. She didn't want a doctor to look too closely.

'I think it's too deep for that. But the doctor can have a look; we can let him decide.'

Penny covered the wound with gauze and a temporary bandage. 'That should hold it for now.' Blood and saline had soaked into the protective cover. Penny bundled it up and threw it away before replacing it with a fresh sheet.

'How many doctors are there?' Ella asked.

'Just one. Why?'

Penny had said 'we can let him decide'. She didn't want a male doctor. 'I'd prefer a female doctor.'

'This isn't the city, love, we're lucky to have a doctor at all,' Penny told her. 'I'm pretty sure it's going to need stitches if you want it to heal. So, shall I call him?'

Ella hesitated but her leg was throbbing and she knew it needed to be treated. She'd be no good to Liv if she let it get infected. She nodded.

'All right, then,' Penny said. 'I'll give him a ring and then I'll make you both a sandwich while you wait.'

'You don't need to do that,' Ella protested. 'But a glass of water would be lovely.'

Penny took a paper cup from a stack on the bench and filled it with water from the tap at the sink. 'It's no trouble,' she said as she passed Ella the cup. 'Just a cheese and Vegemite sandwich. What do you think, Olivia? Would you like that?'

Liv nodded as Ella's stomach rumbled, protesting loudly, as she sipped the water.

'Sounds like you could do with a feed too,' Penny commented. 'Do either of you have any allergies?'

Ella shook her head.

'Why don't you come with me, Olivia? You can give me a hand and let your mum have a little rest.'

Ella wondered if she should resist and keep Liv with her, but she was so tired, and the thought of having a few moments to herself—even if it was while she was stuck on a treatment plinth waiting for a doctor she didn't want to see—was an opportunity she couldn't pass up. It wasn't often she had a minute to herself. She closed her eyes as Penny closed the door.

Her mind whirled, running through the events of the past hour as she wondered what it meant for them. She had planned to rest here for a few days before continuing to Queensland, but now she was without a car. How would they get there?

She had insurance, but she had no idea how long a claim would take to get processed, and had she insured for replacement value, or more? She didn't know what her car was worth but it probably wasn't much. Would the pay-out be enough to buy her something decent—something that would make the two-thousand-kilometre trip to Queensland?

'Here you go.'

Ella woke with a fright when Penny and Liv returned. Penny was carrying two plates, each with a sandwich and half an apple on it. She put one on the desk for Liv and passed the other one to Ella. 'This one's for you; it'll do you the world of good. Dr Donato is on his way but I'll leave you two to eat while I take care of a few things.'

'Will you come back when the doctor gets here?' Ella could hear a slight note of hysteria in her voice but she didn't want to be left alone with the doctor.

Penny was in the doorway but she glanced over her shoulder, looking at Ella. Had she picked up on it too? She nodded and answered, 'Yes, I'll be back.'

Ella had washed her hands, devoured her sandwich and was just finishing the apple when Penny walked back into the room. This time she carried an armful of clothes, which she laid on the end of the treatment plinth.

Ella frowned. 'What's all this?'

'You and Olivia need to get out of your clothes. They're wet, muddy and ripped. You can have a look through this pile and see what fits.'

'Where did they come from?'

'We keep a cupboard of donated items. You'd be surprised how often we need a change of clothes. People are sick on themselves or kids come in after falling off their bikes and their clothes are torn or bloodied. I don't have any spare shoes, though. I'll have to get some for you.' She handed Ella a container of wet wipes. 'You can use these to clean some of the mud off you before you get changed.'

Ella rifled through the pile as Penny left, closing the door behind her. She found a pair of shorts and a T-shirt that would fit Liv and helped her to put them on before she looked through the pile again, searching for something for herself.

There was a sleeveless summer dress. She put that back in the pile—it was pretty but far too revealing. There was a skirt, a T-shirt, a pair of lightweight cotton trousers and a button-up shirt. Had Penny chosen those last two items deliberately? They were an unusual choice, considering the temperature. Did Penny have suspicions? Had she picked them out to give Ella on option that would provide some coverage? And would Ella be confirming those suspicions by choosing to cover up?

Ella didn't know the answer, but these items were just what she needed, and she put them to one side before she stripped off her shirt and skirt. She gave her skin a quick rub with the wet wipes to remove some of the caked-on river mud before pulling on the trousers and shirt. She couldn't worry about Penny. Whatever she surmised from Ella's choice of clothing was irrelevant—there was no way Ella was going to wear anything that revealed her arms.

She buttoned up the shirt and threw her ruined skirt into the bin next to the sink but kept her old top and Olivia's clothes. They could be washed. There was a small mirror above the sink and Ella laughed wryly as she caught sight of her reflection. Despite the clean clothes, she was a mess. Her face was still streaked with mud and her hair was tangled. She'd lost her shoes and was dressed in second-hand clothes without even a hairbrush to her name. She didn't know why she'd thought her luck might change. At this point, it seemed as though it had certainly run out.

She grabbed a wet wipe and ran it over her face, removing as much of the dirt as she could, before turning her attention to her hair. She tried to tease some of the tangles from it before giving up just as there was a knock on the door.

It opened a crack and Penny stuck her head in. 'Are you decent?'

Ella nodded and the door opened wider, admitting both Penny and a man who looked very much like Luke but, instead of wearing old shorts and a T-shirt, he was dressed in blue hospital scrubs. He must be Luke's identical twin, Ella decided.

He smiled at her as he crossed the room and Ella's heart skipped a beat.

She'd wondered what Luke would have looked like if he'd cracked a smile. She'd thought he was handsome but this version of him—this tall, smiling version—was breath-taking.

Caught unawares by her reaction, she was about to smile back when he said, 'Ella, you gave in.'

Ella frowned. He recognised her—so, not Luke's identical twin, then. Just Luke.

'What are you doing here?' she asked as her brain tried to process the turn of events. Her thought processes felt delayed. A lack of sleep, lack of food, stress, shock, adrenalin, or a combination of all of the above, was making her brain foggy.

'I'm the doctor.'

CHAPTER THREE

HE WAS THE DOCTOR?

Ella's reasoning was taking time to catch up to her vision. The scruffy, brusque, albeit calm and attractive man who had turned up in his dinghy to rescue her was the doctor?

'You didn't say anything in the boat,' she accused.

'Would it have made any difference? I wasn't sure you were going to take my advice. But it's good to know you've got some common sense,' he continued.

'What's that supposed to mean?' Ella bristled.

'Flood water is notoriously filthy. The last thing you want is an infection. Best to get any cuts cleaned up and treated.' He had his back to her as he stood at the sink and washed his hands.

He was tall and he had to stoop over the sink. She looked at the broad expanse of his shoulders and his long legs, lean hips. When he'd arrived in his little boat she'd assumed, swayed by both his muscular build and his clothing, that he was a labourer or a farmer. A man who did a physical job. She would never have picked him as a doctor.

He reached up to pull paper towel from a dispenser on the wall. She looked at his hands. At his long fingers. She'd noticed his soft, clean hands in the boat but hadn't paid attention. They should have been a giveaway that perhaps her first impressions had been inaccurate.

She watched him dry his hands but her attention was diverted to Penny who was having a conversation with Liv while she prepared equipment for Luke. She hoped Penny didn't get too much information out of her daughter. Pre-schoolers could, unwittingly, be a font of knowledge, divulging all sorts of secrets.

'How old are you, Olivia?'

'I'm going to be five soon. How many sleeps, Mummy?'

'Fifteen more,' Ella replied. Liv turned five on the same day Ella turned twenty-six. She had been Ella's twenty-first birthday gift.

'Wow, that's not far away. You must be getting excited,' Penny said.

Please don't ask if she's having a party, Ella thought.

Liv had never had a party. Ella had no family

and, by the time Liv was old enough to invite friends, Ella had avoided the topic. She hadn't wanted to negotiate hosting a party, not knowing what might trigger her ex's mood. She and Liv had kept to themselves. She'd been a stay-at-home mum for two years. Liv had gone to kindergarten but Ella hadn't fostered any friendships with the other parents. She hadn't volunteered at the kindy; she hadn't been involved. It was easier that way. And now, stuck in this small town, halfway between their old life and their new one, they had no one to invite.

'You'll be starting school soon, then,' Penny continued as Liv nodded.

Ella relaxed. School was something they had talked about. That was one reason she was making this move. She wanted a fresh start and she hadn't wanted to enrol Liv in a school where people already knew, or thought they knew, their business. Making this move was hard but it would be harder if Liv had been happy and settled in school. Ella would have felt guilty about pulling her out if she'd made friends.

'All right, Ella, let's have a look.' Luke was talking to her. She turned her attention back to him, still trying to reconcile the scruffy first impression with this current version. He was clean-shaven, but he had been before: she could recall the strong line of his jaw. But a simple change of clothes had made a huge difference to his appearance. Whereas before, in the boat, he'd appeared relaxed and capable, he now looked neat, efficient and competent. She wished a change of clothes had the same effect on her but she suspected she still looked a dishevelled mess.

His hands reached for the hem of her trousers and Ella quickly pulled the loose leg up above her knee, keeping one hand on the fabric to hold it close against her thigh. She didn't want him to lift it any higher; she didn't want to expose her bruises. They were fading slowly, changing colour from purple to yellow after a week, but they were still obvious on her pale skin.

'Let's get this bandage off.' She was tense but his hands were gentle. She recalled how he'd lifted Liv, how his quiet voice had soothed her. She couldn't imagine him yelling or hurting anyone. Doctors took an oath, didn't they, to do no harm?

He unwound the bandage from her calf and fresh blood ran down her leg as he removed the gauze. Penny was there, ready to mop up.

'Yep, I reckon a couple of stitches will pull this together nicely. I'll give you a local anaesthetic just to numb the area.' He held a piece of clean gauze against the wound while Penny drew up the anaesthetic.

'This might sting a little.'

Ella turned her head away, not wanting to watch the injection being administered, or wanting to look at Luke. She was frightened and emotional and worried she'd burst into tears if someone showed her kindness.

'Are you up to date with a tetanus shot?' he asked as he waited for the anaesthetic to take effect.

'Yes. I had one at the same time as Liv.'

'Good. Let's get you stitched up.'

Ella closed her eyes as Penny handed Luke the needle and thread.

'All done.' She opened her eyes to find the wound covered by a dressing. 'You'll need a course of antibiotics just to be on the safe side.'

She lifted her eyes to meet his, amazed again how the colour of his scrubs made his blue eyes even more hypnotising.

'Is the pharmacy open today?' Pelican's Landing was a small country town. She didn't expect the pharmacy to be open on a Sunday.

'No, it will be closed until tomorrow. I'll give you enough tablets for a couple of days and a prescription to take to the chemist for more. A five-day course should be enough but I'll need you to come back after that for me to check the wound,' he said as he applied a waterproof dressing over the stitches. 'You can shower with the dressing on but no swimming or taking baths— you don't want to soak it.'

She swung her legs over the side of the bed and stood up. Black spots danced before her eyes and the room swayed. She closed her eyes and groped for the bed to steady herself while the dizziness eased. Her hand found fresh air as she felt her knees buckle.

But before she hit the floor she felt hands grip her elbows, stopping her fall. She tensed, her body automatically responding to the unexpected pressure of a pair of hands on her body. She waited for the pressure to increase, waited for the hands to squeeze her arms, waited for the discomfort. But, instead of the hands tightening their grip, she felt them release her and then an arm wrapped around her back, supporting her. She opened her eyes, her vision clearing, to find Luke watching her closely with his blue-eyed gaze. He had caught her and continued to hold her as she regained her equilibrium. She was leaning into him. He was solid and firm but his hands were gentle as he supported her. She let herself be held momentarily before she came to her senses and pulled away.

So much for standing on her own two feet—the first slight hiccough and she was fantasising about being able to lean on someone, about having someone to shoulder some of her worries.

She backed away, only to find herself trapped between Luke and the bed. She leant against the edge of the plinth. It was better to let the bed support her than to lean on Luke.

'I think you should lie down again.'

'I'm fine. I just stood up too quickly.'

'Let me check your blood pressure before you go, just to be on the safe side.'

'I'm fine, really.'

'Humour me,' he said as he scooped up her legs and lifted them back onto the bed, before reaching out to pick up a sphygmomanometer.

Ella was emotional, close to tears. *Get a grip*, she admonished herself.

She'd always had an active imagination and had always been able to retreat into fantasy. It was an escape, a preservation technique, but lately she hadn't been able to do that. Real life had taken over. Responsibilities and motherhood meant she couldn't afford to daydream any more. Now she had to deal with reality, and the simple reality was she had been planning to start over. Now she would have to start from scratch. And there was a difference between the two. A big difference. And she couldn't expect anyone else to help her. There was no one else. She couldn't let a moment of kindness weaken her. She had to manage on her own.

Before she had time to react he'd slid her sleeve up and his fingers were on her wrist, feeling for her pulse.

She knew he would see the bruises but she had no way of hiding them. She waited for him to say something but he kept silent as he wrapped the cuff around her arm and inflated it.

'Your blood pressure is okay. Have you eaten today?'

'Yes, Penny made us both a sandwich.'

'What brings you to Pelican's Landing? Are you visiting friends?'

Ella shook her head. 'No, just passing through.'

'You're travelling on your own? Just the two of you?'

She nodded, wondering if this was his way of getting information about her background? About her bruises?

'You don't know anyone in town?'

'No. We are on our way to Queensland—we just stopped here for a few nights to break up the trip.'

'On your way from where?'

'Western Australia.'

'Well, you won't be able to go back to the caravan park.'

She wasn't stupid, she knew that. Her situation was getting more dire by the minute. She'd taken Liv and fled Geraldton with the bare minimum, just what she could fit into her car, and now she had lost everything. She had nothing left and nowhere to go.

'You'll need somewhere to stay.'

'I've spoken to Sam,' Penny said. 'He told me the SES are setting up emergency accommodation at the community hall. I can take Ella and Olivia up there and see what's been organised.'

'I guess that's a good place to start. Is that okay, Ella?'

Ella was too tired, too emotionally spent to problem-solve, and it didn't sound as if she had any other option. There wasn't going to be a knight in shining armour coming to her rescue. This was real life, not a fairy tale, but unfortunately for her and Liv their life appeared to be one drama followed closely by another. And she didn't want to deal with any more dramas today. She *couldn't* deal with any more; she didn't have the energy.

If Penny could get them to the hall, it would be one less thing for Ella to think about.

She'd worry about tomorrow, tomorrow.

She nodded and said, 'I appreciate your help, Penny, thank you.'

* * *

Ella collapsed onto a chair in front of the general store. She was exhausted. She appreciated that the community of Pelican's Landing had organised temporary accommodation for the caravan park guests who had been so unceremoniously forced from their sites, but the accommodation was basic at best, and she'd slept fitfully. Liv had been wiped out by the events of the day and, despite sleeping on a gym mat covered by a light sheet, she'd fallen asleep quickly. Ella, on the other hand, had not. But it hadn't been physical discomfort that had kept her awake. The gym mat was thick enough, and the night was warm, but being housed in a hall full of strangers had Ella on edge.

While some of the other faces were familiar to her from the caravan park, she didn't know any of the other people. She'd nodded and said hello in passing over the previous two days, but she hadn't really spoken to them, and she was nervous. She felt as though she'd slept with one eye open, looking for threats, prepared to flee at the first sign of danger. People had been quiet, silent, frightened but they were still strangers, traumatised and upset. They'd all been through the same experience, but there was no sense of bonding, and Ella had been wary.

She had spent the morning in town, Liv trailing beside her, as she investigated their options for accommodation. Volunteers from the State Emergency Service, the local council and a local charity had arrived early in the day to get people's details and ostensibly assist them with finding temporary accommodation. Ella had been optimistic at first but her hopes had quickly been dashed. There was a rental crisis with no vacancies in the district—never mind in Pelican's Landing—and she couldn't afford the holiday accommodation in the motel, pubs and bed and breakfast. The council was planning to contact shack owners who didn't live permanently in Pelican's Landing to see if they would offer their holiday homes for temporary accommodation but Ella couldn't pin her hopes on that. The message seemed to be that their best bet was to stay with family and friends—but Ella didn't have any.

She'd also visited the tourist information centre to enquire about other caravan parks in the region. Her car was submerged, and her tent and their meagre belongings were god knew where, so Ella's only option was to find a park on the bus route from Pelican's Landing that had a cabin to rent. The lady in the office had booked her a cabin in a town across the border in Victoria but the bus wasn't coming until Thursday.

Ella let out a sigh as she contemplated three more nights in the community hall. She'd dropped her prescription for antibiotics at the pharmacy and then bought Liv the ice-cream she'd promised her yesterday from the general store next door. She collapsed onto a chair in front of the shop. Her leg was throbbing; she knew she'd walked on it more than she should have today. It felt swollen and sore. She put her foot up on a second chair, while Liv devoured her ice-cream, and tried to ignore the ache. It would be fair to say this move was not turning out as she'd anticipated. She hadn't thought it would be smooth sailing or easy—nothing in her life was—but she had thought it might be a little less dramatic, a little less difficult.

Some people were lucky. But not her. Could you make your own luck? Ella hoped so. Maybe it was her turn. Things could hardly get worse. She was determined to make a better life for her and Liv.

By herself. No one was coming to rescue her—she was well aware of that—and she'd learned that if she wanted things to change it was up to her. She had to have faith in herself. She was on her own but she could do it.

'Ella, hello.' Ella looked up to see Penny standing in front of her, carrying a bag from the pharmacy. 'How are you today?'

Ella thought of all the words she could use to describe her current state. Tired. Overwhelmed. Dejected. Frustrated. But she didn't want to sound like a victim. Or to sound like she wasn't coping. 'We're okay,' she replied.

'You look tired.'

'I didn't sleep well. Being in a room full of strangers was a little unnerving. Hopefully to-night will be better.'

'Do you have to spend another night at the hall? I thought they were looking for something a bit more substantial than mats on the floor?'

Ella nodded. 'Apparently there's an accommo-dation shortage in the area. It doesn't look like there's much the authorities can do. It's impos-sible to conjure beds out of thin air.'

'What will you do?'

'The staff in the tourist office have found me some accommodation in a caravan park in Swan Hill, but my car is somewhere in the river and there's no bus until Thursday, so we'll stay until then.'

Penny's brow creased and Ella could see she

was mulling something over. 'I might know a place that you could stay in for a few days. Why don't you meet me at the clinic at half-past five and I'll make some enquiries?'

'Are you sure?'

'Not a hundred percent, but there's no harm in asking. Bring your things with you in case it works out.'

Ella gave a half-smile. 'I'm not sure that you could call one change of clothes and a tooth-brush "things", but we'll do that. Thank you.' Her spirits lifted. It might not happen but just to know someone cared enough to try to help made a world of difference. She'd accept Penny's offer of help and tomorrow she'd start again. On her own.

Penny put her bag of supplies on the café table and opened her purse. She pulled out some cash and handed it to Ella. 'There's a country Target in the shopping complex up the hill from the scout hall. Why don't you go and get yourselves some essentials?'

Ella shook her head. 'Thank you, but we'll manage.'

'Don't be silly. You can pay me back later if it makes you feel better,' Penny insisted, picking up her bags and refusing to let Ella return the money. 'I'll see you in a couple of hours.'

* * *

'I'm off to see Mrs Macdonald,' Luke said as he stuck his head into Penny's office. His elderly patient had been discharged from hospital in Adelaide following cardiac surgery and he wanted to check on her recovery. 'Call me if anything urgent comes up.'

'Before you go, I needed to ask you something.' Penny waylaid him. 'I bumped into Ella in town earlier. She needs a place to stay for a few nights.'

'What's wrong with the community hall?'

'She's a single mum with a young daughter. She doesn't feel safe there.'

'Did she tell you that?'

'Not exactly. She did say she didn't sleep well because of all the strangers sharing the space. I think she was frightened or nervous, or both.'

'You think she's had some past trauma? In addition to the flood, I mean?' Luke looked at Penny. He'd seen the bruises on Ella's arms and legs, despite her efforts to hide them from view. Should he have questioned her? 'Do you think I should have asked her if she was safe?'

He'd been thrown by his reaction to Ella. Her presence had caused colliding thoughts and conflicting emotions in him. She was stunning but young and he'd felt his reaction to her was inappropriate. She was scared and vulnerable—a patient. A mother and possibly a partner too. But being forbidden didn't stop her from being desirable. There was something special about her that had drawn him in, almost bewitched him. He knew he hadn't been thinking clearly and now he was worried he'd made a professional mistake.

'Ella is obviously wary of men, and it's possible she could be in an abusive relationship or not long out of one,' Penny replied. 'But I don't think we should be jumping to conclusions, and I'm not sure that she was in the right headspace to discuss anything like that after what happened yesterday,' she continued, letting him off the hook.

'She did say she and Olivia were travelling alone so I think, for the moment, she's out of harm's way. She told me she spent the day looking for an alternative place to stay but there's nothing suitable in Pelican's Landing—it's bursting at the seams with displaced people. And she has no means of getting anywhere else, as her car was swallowed by the flood. She's stuck here and she needs somewhere to live. Would you be willing to let her use your cottage? You've been saying for six months you plan to let the cottage to people in the community who need assistance but you haven't done it yet. Why don't you have Ella as your first tenant?'

Luke had converted an old barn on his parents' property into self-contained accommodation for his sister but it had been sitting empty and unused for many years. As Penny rightly pointed out, he had recently toyed with the idea of renting it to locals who needed assistance, but he hadn't actually taken that step yet. And he wasn't sure he wanted Ella living on his doorstep.

Besides, if Ella had suffered some trauma or abuse at the hand of a man, he couldn't imagine she'd feel comfortable staying in his cottage. The converted barn was in close proximity to his home and he was, to all intents and purposes, a stranger to Ella. 'If Ella is wary of men, strangers or otherwise, she'll hardly want to stay at my house,' he said, thinking that was a valid excuse. 'Why don't you have them?'

'I would gladly have them but we're about to start our renovations. We can't take guests at the moment. We're going to have a portable loo and no kitchen.'

'They've been sleeping in a tent. I'm sure they'll be happy just to have proper beds.'

'Which you can offer them,' Penny insisted. 'Along with a kitchenette and bathroom.'

He recognised Penny's tone, and knew he would have difficulty convincing her that her idea was not a sound one, but he wasn't quite sure if he was ready to confront the reality of having someone living in the cottage that had been meant for Gemma. And he was even more cautious about offering it to Ella. Her vulnerability reminded him of his sister and he didn't need a daily reminder of how he'd let his sister down.

'She's not a local in need, though, is she?' he said, trying to find an argument that would hold up to Penny's persistence.

'Think of it as redemption for Gemma.'

That was the trouble with Penny. She'd known him since he'd been born, and she had worked for his father in the clinic before Luke had taken over. Penny knew everything Luke had been through and knew how guilty he felt over what had happened to Gemma. The idea of renting out the cottage had begun as a way of making sense of Gemma's death but that didn't mean Ella was the right first tenant. 'I don't think it's a good idea. I don't know her.'

'That doesn't matter. You always wished someone would help Gemma when you couldn't. You can help Ella. Offer her a kindness—she looks like she could use it.'

Penny was right, he had tried to help Gemma,

but she'd refused his efforts. She'd moved away, probably in order to escape everyone she knew, but that didn't mean someone else might not have been able to get through to her. If only someone else had tried she might still be alive today. And Luke *did* want to help Ella but that didn't necessarily extend to offering her a place to live which was quite literally in his own back yard.

'Can I at least show her the cottage and see what she thinks?' Penny asked. 'She only needs it for a few days.'

He wasn't convinced that having Ella as a neighbour would be a wise decision but he nodded reluctantly, knowing that Penny would keep hounding him until he relented. 'If she wants to see it you can take her up there when you leave here.'

He could only hope Ella wouldn't accept the offer. If she was as wary of men as he suspected, perhaps the option wouldn't appeal to her.

Ella and Liv were at the clinic on time to meet Penny. Luke was nowhere to be seen. Ella found herself partly relieved and partly disappointed.

Penny drove them west out of town but, instead of turning up the hill away from the river, she took a road that followed the curve of the river bank. Ella could see some houses overlooking the water on her left, but the area looked rather agricultural, with plantings of olive groves, fruit orchards and even a few sheep in the paddocks around the houses.

Penny turned left onto a long dirt driveway that ran down towards the river. The driveway ended at a grand two-storey stone house that faced the water. From the back Ella could see wide verandas that ran along both sides of the house, nestled under top floor balconies, and she assumed the verandas continued across the front. The house would have an amazing view over the river. Surely this wasn't the cottage Penny had been talking about? But, just as Ella was about to clarify the offer Penny turned left again, driving behind the house, and came to a stop near another stone building that sat a few hundred feet from the main dwelling.

'Here we are,' Penny said as she switched off the engine, and Ella and Liv climbed out of the car.

It was obvious this building would have once been the barn for the imposing house that sat in front. Chickens scratched in the dirt nearby, catching Liv's attention, but Ella was captivated by the old barn which had been renovated and converted into accommodation. Set back and to the left behind the main house, it still had a view down the gentle slope that stretched away to the river. A small garden had been planted in front of the cottage. Ella could smell mint and rosemary, and spied strawberry plants and cherry tomato bushes, both laden with fruit, sprouting between rose bushes. A small outdoor table and chairs sat underneath a wisteria-covered arbour. It was enchanting.

'It's so pretty,' she said as Penny opened a small metal gate set into the wire fence and Ella followed her along the brick path, through the garden, to the barn door.

Penny pushed the heavy wooden door and stepped inside as it swung wide.

'It wasn't locked?' Ella was surprised and a little worried but, as she turned to close the door behind Liv, she saw it was fitted with a deadlock.

'No,' Penny replied. 'Lots of the locals don't tend to lock up but there will be a key somewhere if you want it.'

Ella looked around the room. The old stone walls had been repointed and the floor tiled. The layout was simple, the furnishings comfortable. There was a living room at one end where a large leather couch, piled high with cushions in neutral colours, faced a pot-belly stove. A sisal rug stretched from the couch almost to the fireplace and a single arm chair was tucked under a window. Straight ahead was a small, round wooden dining table with four ladder-back chairs and beyond that a simple kitchen ran along the back wall. There was a window above the kitchen sink, which looked out onto a grove of olive trees. It was idyllic. Peaceful.

Despite the heat of the day, the room was cool. The thick stone walls of the old stable had kept the heat out, but the air had a musty smell, as if the building had been closed up for a while. Penny whizzed around, opening the few windows in the barn walls to let some fresh air in.

The high-pitched roof had exposed timber beams but at one end of the room, to Ella's right, there was a staircase leading to a mezzanine level.

'Can I go outside and see the chickens?' Liv asked as Ella followed Penny up the stairs to a mezzanine floor, which she guessed had probably been an old hayloft, and which had been converted into a bedroom.

'Yes. But stay inside the garden, don't go through the gate. And don't go near the river.' The lawn around the main house sloped away from the barn down to the river. Ella didn't want Liv anywhere near that water. After what had happened yesterday, she didn't think Liv would be tempted to go near the river, but she was grateful that the cottage was surrounded by a fence.

She checked that the gate was closed before returning to make her way up the stairs to where a large bed, an arm chair and a chest of drawers took up most of the space.

'There's only one bed, I'm afraid,' Penny said.

'That doesn't matter.' After sleeping in her car, in a tent and on the floor of the community hall a bed, any bed, would be a luxury. 'Liv is small; I can easily share with her.'

Ella retreated down the stairs and stuck her head into the bathroom which was tucked under the mezzanine. It was compact but had everything she needed and even a small washing machine. She stepped out and had another look around the living space.

The converted barn was small but she didn't need space. Because of its history as a barn, there were few windows, which Ella saw as a positive. Large windows were a security risk, in her opinion. The only flaw in her mind was that the building only had one external door. If that was blocked, there was no other means of escape.

She tried to relax. She only needed a place to stay for a few days. No one was looking for her. No one knew where she was. She would be safe here.

'What do you think?'

'It's gorgeous. I'd love to stay for a few nights, if you're sure that's all right.'

'Mummy, Mummy, it's Maisie!' Liv's voice interrupted.

Ella wandered out into the garden to find Liv wrapped around a shaggy black-and-white dog. Standing beside the dog was Luke.

Ella frowned. 'Luke, what are you doing here?'

'I've brought you some linen for the cottage.'

Ella was confused. 'Why?'

'This is my cottage.'

'Yours?' Ella looked at Penny, who was squatting down with Liv. Was she avoiding Ella's gaze?

He thrust the pile of linen into her arms before saying, 'Hopefully, that's everything you need. Penny can help you settle in.'

'Penny, can I speak to you for a minute?' Ella asked.

Penny straightened up and said, 'Olivia, why don't you go with Luke to collect the chickens' eggs?'

Ella expected Luke to say he was too busy but he just looked at Liv, waiting for her reply. When she nodded eagerly, Luke gave a whistled command to Maisie and he and Liv wandered off.

Ella wanted to tell her to stay, her natural instinct to protect her daughter rising to the fore, but she had no reason to suspect he had any ulterior motives. He had only shown them kindness so far. But, still, trust was hard for her.

'She'll be all right,' Penny said.

Ella looked at her. How did she know what Ella was thinking? She wanted to ask but she had another, more pressing, question for Penny. She looked at her as Luke retreated. 'Are you sure he's okay with me staying here?'

Penny was staring after Luke, her expression blank. Ella couldn't get a read on what she was thinking but she replied, 'He'll be fine with it.'

That sounded to Ella as though he hadn't offered the accommodation to her but had rather been coerced. And that presented Ella with a dilemma. She didn't want to be a nuisance but she definitely didn't want to go back to the community hall. She was between a rock and a hard place. 'Why didn't you tell me this was Luke's cottage?'

'Does it matter?'

Of course it mattered. She didn't want to owe Luke, or any man, any favours.

'Is that his house too?' she asked, pointing to the large house between them and the river.

'Yes. He lives there.'

'We can't stay here.' Ella was disappointed. The cottage would be perfect for a few days—it was small but plenty big enough for the two of them, it had everything they could need and was a space of their own—but Ella didn't feel comfortable accepting the offer. It would have been an appealing offer if only it didn't belong to Luke. To any man. She wished it were Penny's.

'Why not?'

'I don't want to be reliant on anyone—especially not a man,' she said, trying not to sound ungrateful.

'It's just for a few days and he won't even notice you're here. You don't have a lot of options,' Penny said. 'And I thought you didn't want to go back to the community hall.'

'I don't.'

'He lives in the big house,' Penny said. 'But he's never home. He's a good man,' she added. ''you'll be safe here.'

Ella looked warily at Penny.

'You don't need to tell me anything,' Penny continued. 'All I'm saying is that you'll be safe here. I've known Luke all his life and, even if I hadn't, it's a small town and I'd know anything there is to know. I work with him. I can vouch for him. He's a good man. He's got some baggage but he's calm and gentle. This is a good community. You don't need to stay here for ever, just take some time to catch your breath,' she said as Liv returned.

'Luke said we could have these eggs for dinner,' she said, proudly displaying a bucket which contained half a dozen fresh eggs.

Ella looked past Liv to the door but her daughter was on her own. Luke had disappeared.

'Go on, take those sheets inside.' Penny bossed Ella while she stood there looking out the door. Ella had forgotten all about the pile of linen in her arms. 'I'll grab some things from my car and then come back and help you make up the bed. Stay here tonight and if you change your mind you can look for something else tomorrow.'

Ella knew she was unlikely to find an alternative at this point in time. She could go back to the tourist office and see if there was another option, but it was too late to do that today, and she didn't want to return to the community hall. She wanted to stand on her own two feet but she wasn't going to look a gift horse in the mouth. Even if the gift horse felt like a Trojan horse. That was between Penny and Luke.

If Luke was happy for Ella to stay, she would accept. She was tired and the cottage did have appeal.

She didn't need to cross paths with Luke. She only needed three nights.

CHAPTER FOUR

ELLA KISSED LIV goodnight and turned off the bedside light.

'Come on, Maisie, downstairs now,' she said to the dog, who was curled up on the floor. Maisie had appeared at their door as they'd finished dinner and Liv had cajoled Ella to let her inside. Ella had seen Luke come home—she could see the driveway from the kitchen window—and she'd seen him go out again. She tried not to notice what he was doing, but it was difficult when she could hear his car, and when his dog turned up looking for company.

The dog was well-trained, so she was no trouble, and Liv was besotted with her. Ella didn't mind letting Liv spend time with her, as it was an easy way to keep Liv happy. An easy reward after a couple of trying days.

Ella flicked the kettle on and leant on the kitchen bench, waiting for it to boil. Her leg was throbbing; she and Liv had walked into town earlier to do some errands and buy some groceries and she'd carried home more than she should have. Penny had given her some basic supplies yesterday, obviously expecting Ella to take up the offer of temporary accommodation. She had bread, milk, tea, coffee and cheese in her car which, together with the fresh eggs, had provided dinner for Liv and Ella. But she'd needed to supplement the supplies for another day. Now her calf was swollen, and she was looking forward to a hot shower before hopping into bed, but first she'd have a cup of tea and put her feet up for a minute.

As she dropped a tea bag into her mug, she heard the sound of Luke's car, the throb of the engine and the crunch of the tyres on the dirt driveway. Dusk was falling and his headlights swept across the kitchen window as he negotiated the slight bend at the start of the drive. She poured hot water into her mug and carried it outside.

It was a beautiful evening, warm, and the air was still. She sat at the outdoor table and put her feet up on a spare chair. Maisie lay down beneath the table. Ella knew she should probably open the gate to let her out but, having just sat down, she couldn't summon the effort required to get up again. She'd enjoy the sunset and drink her tea first. From the garden she could see down the sloping block to the river. The setting sun had turned the cliffs on the opposite side of the river glorious shades of orange, gold and pink. She could hear frogs croaking in the distance and a pod of pelicans flew overhead.

It was a beautiful scene, calm and peaceful to look at, serene on the surface. But Ella knew there were all sorts of dangers lurking beneath the calm water: snags, logs, eddies and strong currents. She'd warned Liv about the dangers of the river but she'd still kept a close eye on her today. She thought Liv was old enough to understand the dangers but accidents happened. She wondered if she should fashion a more secure latch for the garden gate but they only had one more day here. She'd stay vigilant.

She hoped that one day she would be able to stop being so anxious, stop looking over her shoulder for trouble, but she knew that day was a while off yet.

'*Maisie!*' Luke's voice, followed by a whistle, cut through the still evening air before Ella saw him round the corner of his house and head towards the driveway.

Maisie's ears pricked up and she leapt to her feet, tail wagging.

'She's at the cottage,' Ella called out, belatedly realising she shouldn't have said anything, because now her words had Luke retracing his steps and heading in her direction. She should have just opened the gate and let the dog run back to her master.

'Sorry about her,' Luke said as he opened the gate to let Maisie out. 'Was she being a nuisance?'

'No,' Ella replied, looking at the dog who was now turning circles at Luke's side, looking up at him adoringly. 'Liv is her biggest fan—I was afraid she was planning on keeping Maisie captive, but she's asleep now, so you get your dog back.'

'Has Liv ever had a dog?' Luke asked.

'No. But she is an animal lover.'

'And you're not?'

'I wouldn't say that, but raising a pre-schooler is hard work some days. I don't think I need a pet to look after too, but I don't mind having Maisie around as long as she's not my responsibility.' If Ella was completely honest, she'd tell him that she found Maisie's presence reassuring. She felt more secure in an unfamiliar place with the dog there. Ella was pretty sure they were safe here but there was no harm in having Maisie around as an extra layer of protection.

'Fair enough. How was your day today, on a

scale of easy to hard?' He smiled at her and the setting sun seemed to lose a bit of its shine, paling against the force of his smile. He was standing on the outside of the fence, leaning against it, separated from her by the wire but still close. The strength of his smile made her want to reach out to him, to move further into his sphere, but she resisted the feeling, dismissing it as nonsensical, and stayed on her side of the fence.

'About middle of the road,' she replied. Not because of Liv; she'd been compliant enough, bribed with the promise of no chores and something fun to do tomorrow. But there were a million unanswered questions hanging over her head that weighed heavily on her, and on top of that her leg was throbbing, which shortened her tolerance and concentration. Funny, though, that she'd forgotten about her leg since seeing Luke.

'Do you have everything you need in the cottage?'

She nodded. 'Yes. Thank you. It's rather gorgeous and so much better than the community hall.'

She sipped her tea as Luke watched. He seemed in no hurry to be on his way.

'Can I make you a cup of tea or a coffee?' Ella asked, feeling obliged to offer. She was drinking her tea, sitting in Luke's garden. If he was in no hurry to head home, she felt she needed to be hospitable.

'I'd love a black coffee, thanks.'

'I was out here watching the sunset. If you want to have a seat, I'll be back in a minute.' Even though the cottage belonged to Luke, she didn't want to ask him in. It was small and he was large and she knew she'd feel a little bit hemmed in if they were alone together in the small space. It didn't matter that Penny had vouched for him, and that Ella trusted Penny: experience had taught her to be wary.

'Do you normally rent this cottage out?' she asked, when she returned with a fresh cup of tea for herself and a coffee for Luke. She put his mug on the table and sat down opposite him, keeping some distance.

'No.'

She'd got that impression, but the cottage was so cute, it would make a perfect bed and breakfast. But maybe he didn't want to be bothered with that. Penny had said he lived alone, and Ella had seen no evidence of a girlfriend or partner or anyone else who might run the accommodation for him, but he didn't elaborate further and she didn't want to pry.

'Why did you let Penny talk you into letting us stay?' She did want to know that much.

'How do you know I didn't offer?'

'It was pretty obvious the idea was spur of the moment, and you didn't seem that keen when you brought the linen over.'

'I've got used to having the place to myself,' he said. 'But I've known Penny all my life and I've learnt from experience that it's usually easiest to do as she suggests.'

'Sam said the same thing today.'

'Sam?'

'My car was swallowed by the flood waters when the levee bank burst. I had to go to the police station to file a report for the insurance claim. Sam knew the whole story of Liv and me staying here for a few days. He said Penny had decided that it was a good decision, and once Penny decided something it usually happened. I did think it was strange that Sam knew all about it until he told me that he is Penny's husband.'

'I'm sure the news would have spread through town anyway, especially as the cottage isn't normally for rent. Everyone knows everyone's business around here. There are no secrets.'

'None?'

'Not many.'

Ella frowned and sipped her tea. Pelican's

Landing was a lot smaller than Geraldton, where she had been living in in Western Australia and she knew about small-town gossip, but she hadn't expected her news to travel so quickly, and to think that the whole town could know about her business within the space of a few days had her worried. She was right to be moving on in a couple of days.

'What's the matter?' Luke asked in response to her expression.

'I don't like people knowing my business. I guess it's just as well we'll be off to Swan Hill on Thursday.'

'Swan Hill, Victoria?'

Ella nodded.

Now he was frowning. 'You're still going on your holiday? You're not going home?'

Ella shook her head. 'We weren't on holiday. I was relocating to Queensland but I thought we'd have few days in Pelican's Landing to break up the trip. Not my best idea,' she said with a wry smile.

'But Swan Hill? Why don't you just stay here in Pelican's Landing?'

'Because there's no accommodation in town. The town is full.'

'You're welcome to stay here for a bit longer than a few days. I don't need the cottage.'

'I appreciate the offer,' she said, even if she thought he didn't really mean it, 'and I appreciate having a few nights here for now but the reason for this move is to make a life for myself and Liv. On my own. I don't want to rely on other people. I want to stand on my own two feet.'

'And how are you planning on getting to Swan Hill without a car?'

'There's a bus that goes on Thursday. The lady in the tourist information office found us a spot in the caravan park, I just had to wait a few days to get there.'

'Well, the offer is there if you change your mind. Or even if you just want to wait until you replace your car.'

'Thank you, but I have no idea how long it will take to get a new car, and Liv is supposed to start school in a couple of weeks. I need to keep moving if we're going to be settled some-where in time for that.' It was a generous offer but Ella didn't want to be beholden to anyone. What if Luke expected something in return? She'd learnt the hard way that gifts came with strings attached and, having barely broken free of the last lot of strings, she wasn't about to get herself into that position again. It didn't matter that Penny trusted Luke, Ella wasn't going to risk repeating her previous mistakes.

Luke's phone beeped with an incoming text message as he finished his coffee. He put his mug on the table and stood up to pull his phone from his pocket.

'Thanks for the coffee, but I need to get going,' he said as he read the message.

'Are you on call?' she asked.

'You could say that. I'm always on call; I'm the only doctor in town,' he said as he slid his phone away. 'Would you like me to leave Maisie in your garden? I can collect her when I get back.'

Did he think she was in danger? She knew he'd seen her bruises but he hadn't asked anything. She wondered if she should tell him what had been going on. She had a sense she could confide in him, but then someone else would know her secrets, her shame, and she didn't want that person to be Luke.

She was making changes, moving forward. She had left her old life behind her and she didn't need to talk about her past, no matter how recent it was. She wanted a clean slate, a new beginning, a chance to be a different person. Stronger. Self-sufficient. Admitting what had happened to her would feel like admitting to being a failure. 'It's fine,' she said. 'She can go with you.' She wouldn't have minded keeping Maisie with her but she didn't want to look weak or needy. She'd go inside and lock the door instead.

Luke left the cottage and Ella in a conflicted state.

She had obviously been the subject of gossip or innuendo in the past. He should have reassured her. He could tell she was concerned about small-town conversations, and he'd had enough experience to know how bad that could be. But there was an up side to a small town and that was that people stuck together, they rallied around when needed. All you had to do was ask for help. But that wasn't something that seemed to sit comfortably with her.

He wanted her to trust him but he sensed her suspicion of people's motives, her distrust of strangers and her preservation of her own space. To gain her trust, he'd have to be careful. He felt protective of her. She was intriguing, captivating, but she was also a stranger, someone who would be gone from his life in a few days. He didn't want to cultivate a relationship—he didn't want to risk letting her down. He'd done that before; he wouldn't do it again.

Confronted with the reality of having someone living in the barn that had been converted for Gemma, even though Gemma had never lived there, had reignited his feelings of loss and guilt. And compounding that were the similarities between Ella and Gemma. Both young, thin and fragile. Was he making it more difficult for himself by having her live, not with him exactly, but in very close proximity? It had nothing to do with her being a patient or not being a local but everything to do with how he'd felt when she'd collapsed into his arms. His reaction to her had been far from familial but he wasn't ready to examine those feelings. It was easier to keep her at arm's length.

But that wouldn't be fair to Ella. She needed assistance and he could offer it. The cottage had been renovated as a refuge for his sister. It hadn't helped Gemma but maybe it could help Ella.

He stopped at the service station to pick up ice-cream before turning into the nursing-home car park, which was deserted at this hour of the night. He should be at home, like all the other sensible people. Sometimes it felt as if he had no life other than work and visiting his father. When he had spare time, he usually took his boat out and went fishing, or water skiing if he could round up a few people, but with the flood that was off the agenda. Perhaps he'd get out on the water soon. According to the reports from upstream, the river would peak in a few days and the flood waters would start to recede—unfortunately not before creating havoc with the levee bank—and a fishing trip might give him some clear head space.

'Hey, Dad, it's Luke.' He switched the radio to classical music as he greeted his dad.

'Luke! Is your mother coming in?'

'Not tonight, Dad, it's Tuesday—she has her craft group.' He'd learnt from experience that it was easier just to make an excuse for his mother's whereabouts rather than explain that she was no longer with them. When his dad was already restless or agitated, that discussion always ended badly. It would either make him more upset or argumentative and Luke didn't want to risk an argument tonight. 'I brought you an ice-cream, would you like that now?'

He unwrapped the ice-cream, which was on a stick, and handed it to his dad. He could still manage to feed himself if cutlery wasn't required.

'I saw John Collins at the pharmacy today,' Luke said. This was a complete fabrication, but his dad had known John since they had first moved to Pelican's Landing as young men—one a doctor, the other the local pharmacist. Luke knew that there would be enough long-term memory for his dad to have a coherent conversation, even if it was irrelevant.

'How did he look?' his dad asked. 'I haven't seen him at the clinic for a while. He must be due to have his cholesterol level checked.'

'I'll get him to make an appointment. He was saying that Sally has just had another baby, so that's grandchild number six.'

John and his wife had five children and several grandchildren, and Luke knew his dad could comfortably run through the list of ailments that they'd experienced, even if they were not current. He knew, once he got his dad talking about old patients, he would talk happily without expecting anything more than a nod or an occasional comment in agreement. He was happy holding court and hearing the sound of his own voice.

Luke occasionally wondered if his dad missed company. Did he still have enough wits about him to know that, if he misbehaved for the staff, they would call Luke who would then come and sit with him and keep him company?

He finished his own ice-cream as he wondered if this was going to be his life. He loved his work, and he didn't normally mind spending time with his dad, but he realised that tonight he'd rather be talking to Ella. He'd rather be with her talking about their days But he listened as his father chatted away and eventually calmed down and allowed Luke to settle him into bed for the night.

He left the nursing home and drove home, pulling in beside his house and walking around the back he checked on the cottage. Maisie greeted him but the cottage was in darkness. He couldn't disturb Ella now. It wasn't particularly late but a knock on the door would most likely frighten her.

He opened the back door of his own house, letting Maisie inside, and flicked on a light. His house usually welcomed him home after a long day. He found the smell of the river and the sight of moonlight on the water relaxed him, and he found comfort in the familiar sounds of the creaking floorboards and rattling windows. Normally it was his sanctuary, but tonight it just felt cold, empty and lonely.

Ella had spent the best part of Wednesday morning completing paperwork for the insurance company. She was confident they would accept her claim, but they hadn't said how long it would be before she was likely to get the money to buy another car. She had no funds of her own to use so she had to wait for the claim to go through and in the meantime, they were going to have to rely on public transport. Which was non-existent in Pelican's Landing.

Maybe she shouldn't move to Swan Hill tomorrow. Even though there was accommodation available, would she be able to get to where she needed? Perhaps they'd be better off heading straight to Queensland. They could travel by bus—it was a long way, but once they arrived she might have more options for accommodation, transport and even finding a second-hand car in a bigger town. She really didn't know which was her best option and her head was pounding as she tried to work it out.

She sighed. She needed a break from decision-making—or attempted decision-making—and she'd promised Liv they would do something fun in exchange for the time Liv had spent traipsing around doing errands over the past two days and now waiting for Ella to complete all the paperwork. There was an adventure playground at the top of the hill coming into town. It was an uphill walk from Luke's cottage, but not too far, and she knew Liv would enjoy it.

Five minutes after arriving at the playground, Liv was in her element, exploring the gigantic wooden pirate ship that dominated the park. It sat on a large mound and had tunnels running up through the hill into the hold, climbing nets strung from the masts, a ladder to a crow's nest—which thankfully wasn't that high—and even a plank to walk, which ended in a fireman's pole to the ground. At the bottom of the pole there was a choice between a large slippery dip or a flying fox to traverse the rest of the mound down to the picnic area.

Ella sat at a picnic table under a shade sail and tried to let her mind go blank as she kept an eye on Liv, who had already befriended a couple of children, a boy and a girl of similar age. The boy was a little more adventurous than the girls and, after climbing to the crow's nest, he was now encouraging the girls to walk along the plank. The plank was really more of a bridge but the suggestion was there. It had hand rails, with marine-wire sides preventing children from falling off, but it was the pole at the end that made Ella nervous. She'd never liked fireman's poles. She always had visions of the pole being too far away to reach safely and children plummeting to the ground. She had left the picnic table and was halfway up the slope when Liv reached the end of the plank. Before she could remind her to be careful, Liv had grabbed the pole and was sliding down with no problems.

'Are you having fun?' Ella asked, curbing

her concerns when she met Liv at the bottom of the pole.

Liv nodded, a broad grin plastered across her little face. 'Can I try that next?' she said, pointing at the flying fox, where her two new friends were now standing.

Ella watched as the little boy went first again. The flying fox was more like a flying swing. Rather than children reaching overhead and hanging on with their hands there was a small seat at the end of the rope. The little boy sat on the seat, wrapped his legs around the rope and flew down the short slope of the hill. Ella wasn't convinced the flying fox was a good idea, but Liv had been so well-behaved all day she didn't have the heart to argue.

It wasn't an overly long distance, and she reckoned Liv should be able to cling on to reach the bottom. They wandered over to the flying fox as the little boy ran back up the hill, pulling on the rope to drag the seat back up behind him.

'This is Chloe, Mum, she's five.' Liv introduced Ella to the little girl who was waiting for a turn. Ella watched as Chloe successfully managed to fly down the hill. That she was much the same age as Liv reassured her a little, and when she brought the contraption back to the top Ella held the rope steady while Liv sprang onto the seat.

Liv didn't wait for instructions—she'd obviously been watching the other kids. She wrapped her skinny legs around the rope and crossed them at the ankles. Ella gave Liv a little push—not hard, just enough to get her moving—and ran down the hill beside her, keeping one hand outstretched, prepared to grab the rope to slow it down if Liv picked up too much speed. Liv was only a lightweight so she didn't go terribly fast but Ella had forgotten about her own injury and, as she jogged down the hill, keeping pace beside Liv, she felt the wound in her calf pulling.

'Can I do it again, Mummy? That was fun!' Liv asked when they reached the bottom.

'I'm not sure that I can run down the hill again, Liv.' Ella wasn't sure her calf would withstand a second turn.

'Please, Mummy,' she begged. 'I can do it by myself.'

She was probably right—the other children had managed. Liv hadn't gone fast: the incline wasn't steep and Liv wasn't heavy. Ella hadn't needed to control the swing. There was no reason to think she couldn't have a go on her own so Ella relented and together they walked back up the hill, pulling the swing behind them. Ella held it as Liv jumped on for the second time before giving her a gentle push.

She stayed at the top of the hill as Liv swung down the ride. Liv was halfway down the slope when Ella saw her start to slip sideways. She waited for her to correct herself, but her feet had uncrossed, and Ella gasped in fear as her daughter's bottom slipped off the seat. As Ella started to run, Liv tumbled from the seat and landed heavily on her side. Ella's calf screamed in protest as she sprinted down the hill.

'Olivia!'

Liv didn't move. Ella reached her side and knelt in the patchy grass. The ground was hard under her knees, baked by the summer sun. She put her hand on Liv's face. Her eyes were closed but she was breathing—Ella could see her little chest rise and fall.

'Liv? Can you hear me? Liv!'

CHAPTER FIVE

'LIV?' ELLA REPEATED. 'Can you hear me?'

Olivia's eyes remained closed.

'Don't move her. She hit her head when she fell.'

Ella turned round at the sound of a woman's voice. It was another mother, who Ella had seen sitting at a picnic table while her children played.

Ella turned back to her daughter. 'Olivia?' she repeated. Her heart raced as fear and panic overcame her, but she reluctantly heeded the woman's advice, resisting the urge to scoop Liv up, worried now that Liv had sustained a serious injury.

'Olivia?' she said for the third time, hearing her daughter's name catch in her throat as tears threatened to overflow. What had she been thinking, letting Liv ride the flying fox on her own? Maybe those other children had played on it a hundred times before; maybe they'd known exactly what they were doing.

Liv's eyes opened and Ella could breathe again.

'Liv, can you hear me? Are you okay?' she asked. Liv's eyes had a glazed sheen, as if she was having trouble focusing. 'I'm right here, darling. Are you hurt? Can you move your feet and your fingers?'

Liv opened and closed her fists as her eyes slowly regained focus.

'You should take her to the doctor to get her assessed,' the other woman advised, just as Chloe, the little girl Liv had befriended earlier, arrived at her side. This woman must be Chloe's mother. 'She hit her head pretty hard. Do you want me to help you carry your things to your car?' she offered.

'I don't have a car. We walked here.' Ella knew there was only one doctor in town and, while Luke's house was in walking distance, the clinic wasn't, even if Liv could walk on her own.

'I can give you a lift if you like,' the other woman said.

'What happened, Mummy?' Chloe asked at the same time as Ella said,

'Really?'

'Of course. It's no problem,' she said to Ella. 'Just let me round up Jack.' She turned to Chloe and said, 'Chloe, darling, can you fetch Jack?

Tell him we need to go in a hurry. I'll bring you back here after we drive Olivia to the doctor.'

Chloe ran off as the woman waited with Ella. 'I'm Hayley, by the way.'

'I'm Ella,' she replied with a smile. 'And a lift would be brilliant if you're sure it's no trouble.'

Ella waited for Hayley to gather her kids and their stuff and then she carried Liv to Hayley's car. Liv felt heavier than normal and Ella realised it was because she wasn't clinging onto her. She seemed lethargic and unfocused and Ella was trying hard not to freak out.

'Do you need some help to get her inside?' Hayley asked when she pulled up in front of the clinic.

'No, I'll manage. Thank you so much for the lift.'

'No problem. No doubt we'll bump into you again,' Hayley said as Ella picked Liv up and pushed the car door closed with her hip.

Hayley drove off with a wave as Ella carried Liv inside. It was getting late in the day and Ella hoped Luke was still in the clinic. What if he'd been called out to an emergency or was doing a home visit? She was momentarily relieved to see three people in the waiting room; at least that meant Luke was around. But then she realised she was at the end of a queue of patients, and

Ella hoped she didn't have to wait too long. She was worried about Liv. Did this qualify as an emergency? Would Luke let her jump the queue? Liv was conscious and coherent now. She'd probably have to wait her turn.

Penny was behind the reception desk, chatting to a younger woman who was sitting at a computer.

'Ella! I didn't know you had an appointment today,' she said as Ella approached, still carrying Liv.

'We don't. But Liv had an accident at the playground. She hit her head quite hard and blacked out for a bit. I was hoping Luke could take a look at her?'

Liv had her head buried against Ella's shoulder but she stirred in her arms as Ella stood at the front desk. Ella initially thought it was being moved that made her stir until she said, 'I don't feel well, Mummy. I feel sick.'

'Come with me,' Penny said, 'I'll put you straight in a room.'

Ella followed Penny down a passage way and into an examination room. She put Liv down on the bed and stood beside her. Penny handed Ella a green plastic bowl. 'You might want to keep this handy,' she said. 'I'll let Luke know you're here.'

Penny left the door open, returning in a few minutes to check on them. She handed Ella some forms to complete while she waited and said, 'Luke won't be long.'

Ella had just started on the forms when Liv vomited. She was crying—she hated vomiting. 'My head hurts.' Ella turned on the tap and filled a paper cup with water, holding it to Liv's lips.

'Have a sip of water to rinse your mouth out,' she told her. 'And then spit it into the bowl.'

Ella was carrying the bowl back to the sink when Luke came into the room, closing the door behind him.

'Hello, Ella, hello Liv—I hear you've taken a tumble,' he said, directing his statement to Liv before turning to Ella. 'What happened?'

Ella's heart skipped a beat as Luke looked at her. Each time she saw him she was surprised again at how good-looking he was and how confident he was in himself. His confidence reassured her. 'We were at the adventure playground, the one with the pirate ship—do you know it?' Luke nodded and Ella continued, 'She was on the flying fox but she came off and hit her head on the ground. She fell hard. We think she knocked herself out.'

'We?'

'There was another mum there—she saw Liv fall too. She drove us here.'

'How long was Liv out for?' Luke wanted to know.

'I'm not really sure.' It had felt like a lifetime but in reality she knew it hadn't been too long. Ella had said her name three times, relatively quickly. 'Probably less than a minute,' she said. 'But she's just vomited and is complaining of a headache.'

'Do you remember what happened, Liv?'

'No.'

'Do you remember what you had for lunch today?'

Liv looked blankly at Ella. 'A Vegemite sandwich,' Ella answered for her.

'Do you remember my name?' Luke asked.

Liv shook her head.

'I'm Luke. Do you remember I have a dog?'

Liv smiled now and said, 'Yes! Maisie,' and Ella's worry eased slightly.

'That's right,' Luke said, before turning to Ella. His eyes were very blue but somehow still managed to convey a feeling of warmth. 'Has she had a concussion before?'

'No.' Ella had. She'd been hit in the head many times but she'd always protected Liv. She hoped Luke wasn't judging her parenting; she felt bad enough already, and she was relieved that Hayley had been there to witness Liv's accident.

She watched and listened as he checked Liv. Some of his questions seemed difficult and she didn't blame Liv for not being able to answer—what four-year-old knew what day of the week it was? Every day was the same when you were four.

'I'm going to tell you five words now, Liv.' Luke had moved on to another task. 'And then I'm going to ask you to repeat them back to me: elbow, apple, carpet, saddle, bubble,' he said, talking slowly and leaving gaps between the words, before asking her if she could tell him the days of the week, going backwards from Sunday. Liv couldn't do that but she was able to repeat some numbers in reverse order.

Ella wondered if he'd forgotten about the five words he's asked Liv to remember but, before she could ask about that test, he had moved on from what Ella assumed were comprehension tests to some more physical ones.

He checked Liv's eyes and felt her neck, which Liv said wasn't sore, before getting her to take her shoes off and stand up. He had a lovely manner with Liv and Ella found herself softening towards him even more. There were definitely some kind, gentle people in the world and it seemed as though he was one of them. Penny might have been right when she said he could be trusted.

'All right, Liv, stand with your feet together and put your hands on your hips. Like this,' he said as he stood up too and demonstrated what he meant. 'Good. Now, close your eyes. I'm going to count to see how long you can stand still, okay?'

Liv glanced at Ella, a look of concern on her face. Ella nodded, encouraging her to follow Luke's instructions. Liv closed her eyes and after twenty seconds Luke got her to open them, change her foot position to one foot in front of the other and close her eyes again. Liv completed both tests easily.

'Great, well done. Now, do you remember those five words I told you before? Can you tell me what any of them were? In any order.'

'Bubble and apple,' Liv responded. 'I can't remember the others.' She looked at Ella again, obviously wondering if she'd done something wrong.

'Good job, Liv, you did well,' Luke reassured her. 'You can put your sandals back on, if you like; we're all done.'

He had a natural rapport with Liv that pleased Ella. She was well aware that Luke lived alone but she wondered if he had children of his own. Perhaps he was divorced and any children were with his ex. He'd said he was familiar with the playground. She wanted to ask but didn't want to pry.

'I think she'll be okay,' he said as he turned to Ella. 'I'll give her some paracetamol and then you can take her home. Give her a light supper and water to drink then lots of rest for the next twenty-four hours. If you want to wait, I've just got to see the last couple of patients and then I can drop you off before my nursing home visit.'

Ella had been relying on the kindness of strangers more over the past three days than she ever had before, despite her plan to stand on her own two feet. But she didn't relish the idea of walking back to the cottage, possibly having to carry Liv as well, so she nodded gratefully.

Ella heard Luke's car returning not long after she'd put Liv to bed. Luke had dropped them back to the cottage, carried Liv inside and then left for the nursing home. Ella expected him to take the driveway directly to his house and was surprised to hear his car pull to a stop in front of the cottage. She unlocked the door and opened it as he stepped through the gate.

'Hi.'

'Hi, I'm not disturbing you, am I?' he asked as he walked up the path through the garden. 'I just thought I'd check on Liv,' he added after she shook her head.

'She seems fine,' Ella told him. 'She's sleeping.'

'Did she eat?'

'Just some toast.'

'And how about you? How are you?' he asked.

'I'm okay.' Was he worried about her emotional state? 'I had a shock but I'm okay now that Liv seems fine.'

'What about your leg?'

Ella frowned. 'My leg? Why do you ask?'

'You were limping when you walked to my car.'

'Oh. I ran to Liv when she fell; it was a bit sore but I'm sure it's all right.'

'Would you like me to take a look at it for you?'

'It'll be fine; you've had a long day already.' Ella knew her calf hadn't fared too well in the events of the afternoon but she didn't want to be an imposition.

'All my days are long. I think being a doctor is a lot like being a parent. I can't switch off, not completely; there are always one or two patients who concern me. Much like a troublesome child, or any child, I imagine.'

'I don't want to be the troublesome child.'

He smiled at her and she could feel herself relenting. 'You're supposed to come to the clinic for a check tomorrow anyway. Wouldn't it be easier to do it now?'

'We're off to Swan Hill tomorrow; I can get it looked at there.' She tried one last time to stay firm, knowing that letting him look at her calf would mean inviting him in. She knew her resistance was more about being wary of having him at close quarters than about imposing on him.

'Even more reason for me to do it today. It will only take a minute.'

'Are you sure you don't mind?'

'I don't mind. I'll need to change the dressing, so I'll grab my bag from the car and see you inside.'

She sat at the kitchen table and put her foot up on another chair. She thought about putting something she could use as a weapon close to hand—a kitchen knife or a heavy pot—but then she thought about how that would look. What would Luke make of that if he noticed? It would look as if she didn't trust him. If she wasn't going to trust him now, after the past three days when he'd done nothing to suggest she shouldn't, when would she?

Luke returned, carrying a large medical bag, which he left by her side before going to wash his hands in the bathroom. He returned and pulled a chair over to sit near her feet. He peeled off the waterproof dressing that he'd applied over her calf. 'You've pulled some of the stitches,' he said as his fingers ran along the wound.

His hands were warm and gentle and Ella could feel her heart racing. 'But they're still holding.'

'They are, but it will take longer to heal and you'll have a bigger scar. I should be able to pull it together with some Steri-Strips.'

'I wanted those in the first place.'

'Well, now you get your wish.' He smiled at her as he replied and her heart skipped a beat.

She was about to drop her gaze, afraid he might see the effect he was having on her, afraid of how he made her feel. But he had already looked away, ducking his head to open his medical bag, remaining professional and seemingly unaware of the power of his smile.

He found Steri-Strips and another waterproof dressing. He pulled the edges of her wound together and taped the Steri-Strips across it.

'I can do this bit,' Ella said as Luke peeled

open the sleeve containing another waterproof dressing. His touch was beginning to feel intimate. It was unsettling her now.

He looked at her quizzically. 'So can I,' he replied, 'And my hands are clean. Life is easier if you let people help you.'

She wasn't used to people helping her. She didn't want it, nor did she expect it. 'I don't want to rely on anyone else. I want to stand on my own two feet.'

'I'm not suggesting you can't manage, and it's not a case of relying on people—it's just accepting help. They're not necessarily the same thing.'

Either way, she was determined to manage on her own. Determined to do better for Liv.

Oh, God, Liv…! She caught her breath as a thought hit her. Was she doing better for Liv? Liv had a concussion; what if Luke thought it was her fault? Was it? Was it something that needed to be reported?

'Did I hurt you?' Luke was smoothing the edges of the dressing down on her skin but he looked up when he heard her sharp intake of breath.

'No.' She shook her head as she wondered if she should she tell him what was bothering her. What if he'd reported her already? 'You don't have to report Liv's accident, do you?' she asked, deciding she had to know one way or the other.

'To whom?'

'I don't know. Child protection?' she replied as she took her feet off the chair and pushed them under the table.

'No, accidents happen. You weren't responsible, and from what I've seen Liv is well looked-after.' Luke packed his medical kit up, keeping his eyes on his equipment as he asked, 'Have you had any involvement with child protection before? Has Liv been hurt before?'

Ella shook her head.

'But your story is different, isn't it?' He was looking at her now but his tone was gentle, much like his hands.

She dropped her gaze, unable to maintain eye contact. She didn't hear any judgement in his voice but she knew he'd seen her bruises and she couldn't deny his conclusion.

'Ella, it's not something to be ashamed of or embarrassed about. It's not your fault.'

She looked up. 'But that's exactly how I felt— that it was my fault. That I wasn't enough. That I was a failure, I was letting people down.'

'You're not a failure, Ella. I've seen the evidence of the harm that was inflicted on you. I assume it was your partner?' he continued after

Ella confirmed his suspicions with a nod. 'You and Liv have been let down, Ella. Did you ever report the abuse?'

'No.' Ella shook her head. 'I was afraid of what would happen if he found out I'd gone to the police.' Trent had held all the power.

'Does your partner know where you are?'

'*Ex*-partner,' Ella stressed. 'And, no, he doesn't know where we are.'

'And where is he?'

'He's out of the country. He's on a job that means he'll be away for several weeks. It gave me a chance to leave.'

'That was a brave thing to do.'

'I didn't do it for me. I did it for Liv. I was terrified that one day Liv would be in the firing line of Trent's temper. I moved to keep her safe.'

'Do you feel safe here?'

'I'm not sure,' she said honestly. 'I don't re-member what it's like to truly feel safe, and while Trent is still around I'm not sure I'll ever feel completely safe. I can't believe he won't find me.'

'Is he Liv's father? Are you going to have to tell him where you are?'

'No. Liv's father isn't part of our lives.' Ella rarely thought of Liv's father, and certainly not in those terms. He was just the man who'd got her pregnant. He was a backpacker, visiting Australia from Italy and they'd had a brief relationship. She hadn't discovered she was pregnant until he'd left the country. She'd told him about the pregnancy but he hadn't been interested in being a father. He didn't even know if Ella had given birth to a girl or a boy. She'd never heard anything more from him. 'It was just me and my mum when Liv was born. I met Trent when Liv was two.'

'Three years ago?'

'Almost.' She could hear the surprise in his voice and knew he was wondering why she'd stayed so long. Surely he must know it wasn't as simple as walking out a door? 'It wasn't always bad,' she said, hating that she was still making excuses for herself—and, by association, for Trent.

'When I met him, he seemed charming and successful and I was flattered that he would be interested in me, a single mother. I was working in the restaurant at the local marina and taking bookings for berths for visiting yachts. Trent worked as a diesel mechanic in the mines. He was a fly-in fly-out worker, and lots of the miners had boats—cruisers or yachts. They had a lot of money. He worked two weeks on, two weeks off, and I got used to him coming to the restaurant, chatting to me about my life. I started to look forward to seeing him and I admit initially his interest in me was addictive. I never thought he was looking for specific information that made me an easy target, but in hindsight I know that was what he was doing.

'Liv and I moved in to his house and that's when things began to change—all orchestrated by him—but I didn't notice at first. Things were small and gradual, and seemingly inconsequential, and he framed his requests in such a way that he made them seem reasonable.'

'What sort of requests?'

'He asked me to quit my job. He said he'd support me, and because it meant I could stay home with Liv, because it meant she didn't need to go to day care, I said yes. But his real reason, I realised later, was because he didn't want me socialising with anyone. He wanted me isolated. Dependent on him. He tracked my phone, telling me he was worried about my safety, but it was so he always knew where I was and could corroborate my story. If I went out to meet friends, he'd turn up randomly if he was in town, or call them later to check on my story.'

'What about your family?'

She shook her head. 'I haven't seen my father since I was six. He walked out one day and never came back. My mum died when Liv was one. I don't have siblings. It's just me. And Liv. There was no one to worry about me. I've since found out that was one of the things that appealed to him. That it would be easy to manipulate me, to control me. If I'd been stronger, if I'd had a network around me, it would have made things more difficult for him but I was flattered. I had no idea there was such a thing as emotional abuse. I thought he was concerned about me. I thought he loved me.'

She'd justified it initially by telling herself he'd given them a roof over their heads and wasn't she lucky? She was able to stay at home with Liv without having to worry about going to work.

'But when the emotional abuse became physical, I knew I needed to make some changes. If not for my sake, then for Liv's. I didn't want her growing up witnessing that behaviour, or worse, being subject to violence herself.'

'Ella, I'm so sorry this has happened to you. How long was this going on for?'

He reached out a hand to her but she pulled away. She didn't want him to touch her. She couldn't let him cross her boundaries. She was afraid if he showed her sympathy she might crumble. She wasn't looking for sympathy and she didn't want pity, but she wanted him to understand what she'd been through. She knew he'd worked out she'd been a victim of abuse but she didn't want him to think of her as a victim. She wanted him to think she was strong. She realised his opinion of her mattered and she wanted him to know she was a survivor.

Luke withdrew his hand and Ella continued to explain.

'Trent lost his job eighteen months ago. He started drinking daily. When he was working, he'd have a few drinks at the marina, but once he had time on his hands he spent more and more time at the pub. He didn't go to the marina any more—he had to sell his boat and his berth because he couldn't afford to keep it and that infuriated him. He had no savings, he'd been spending everything he earned. He accused me of being a freeloader but he refused to let me get my job back. I was damned if I did and damned if I didn't.

'I said I'd leave. I said I'd never expected him to support me. That was the first time he hit me. He called me ungrateful. I should have left then, but I had nowhere to go, and he swore he was sorry. He said he'd never meant to hurt me, he told me I'd provoked him. He said he'd never hit me again.

'And then he started drinking every day—at

the pub and at home. I had changed the details of the bank account that my single mother's payment went into, so that it went into his account instead. It made me feel like I was contributing. But that came back to bite me. He was spending my money on alcohol.

'I couldn't go back to work, I couldn't leave Liv with him, I was too frightened, and full-time childcare would cost more than I could earn. I was trapped. I couldn't work out how to leave him. If he wasn't at the pub, he was at home. I had no money and it wasn't just me I had to think about. It would have been easier if it was but I needed to get Liv out too.'

Luke was a good listener. It was something she imagined would be a requirement of being a good GP but she was surprised at how the words flowed from her tongue. She'd only known him for three days and it was unlike her to discuss her past with anyone. Was it dangerous to confide in him like this? How would he judge her? What would he think? But it was too late to worry about that now. Besides, she was leaving tomorrow. She'd never see him again.

'Then Trent got a call from someone he used to work with,' she continued. 'They offered him a job on an oil rig. He'd be gone for three months initially, and I realised this was my opportunity to get away. I planned to save some money and then find something to rent but I couldn't access the joint account without him noticing so I needed a job. I managed to call in a favour from someone I knew before I had Liv, and I got a job at the university hub where there was also child care.

'I thought I had it all worked out—but I didn't know that Trent had asked some of his mates to keep an eye on me and one of them told him I was "gallivanting" around town. Trent came back unexpectedly—he'd made up a family emergency—and confronted me. He accused me of cheating on him and became extremely violent. I knew that I couldn't stay in Geraldton; I knew I'd never be safe. I had to run. If I didn't, I was risking my life and Liv's. When Trent left to go back to the oil rig, I packed up my car, took Liv and a few essentials and headed east. That was two and a half weeks ago.'

'That was an incredible effort, Ella; you should be proud of yourself. He hasn't tried to contact you?'

'I assume he has by now but I had I emailed him and told him Liv dropped my phone in the bath. I said I had to get a new one but couldn't afford it so for the time being I wouldn't have a phone. Obviously, I changed my number when I got a new phone, I didn't want him to be able to trace me, but he'll be wondering why he hasn't heard from me by now. Leaving Western Australia was supposed to be our fresh start, and I was prepared for that, but losing the few things that I brought with us, and losing my car in the flood, has just made it that much harder.'

She refused to feel sorry for herself but sometimes it was hard not to get despondent. She sighed. 'I'll just have to start again.'

Luke was watching her carefully and she wished she knew what he was thinking.

'You've done an amazing thing for you and Liv, Ella,' he said. 'The hardest part is walking out the door and not going back.'

'Believe me, I have no intention of going back. I might have only just left my old life behind physically but I moved on emotionally months ago.'

'And you've made it this far all on your own. Will you let us help you now?'

'Us?'

'Me. Penny. Sam. There must be a way we can help. Finding you somewhere permanent to live? A job?'

She shook her head. 'I'm not staying.' She appreciated the offer but she would be leaving in the morning. She'd never see him again.

'Are you still planning on going to Swan Hill tomorrow?' Luke asked, and when Ella nodded he added, 'On the bus?'

'Yes.'

'At the risk of overstepping—and this comes as medical advice—can I suggest delaying your departure for a few days if possible, to give Liv time to recover from her concussion?'

'I thought you said she will be fine.'

'I did. But she still has a concussion and putting her on a bus and travelling six hours is not ideal if it can be avoided. Why don't you wait for the insurance money for your car?'

'Because I don't know how long that will be,' she said.

She should leave. She'd told him more than she needed to—far too much—based on the fact she wouldn't be staying but she didn't want to jeopardise Liv's health. 'I guess I can check the bus timetable and see when the next one goes.' Maybe she could delay just a few days but she didn't want to be an imposition.

'If we're going to stay a bit longer can I at least pay you something for rent? I've been accused of being a freeloader before.' She smiled in an attempt to relieve some of the tension she was feeling.

'No, that's not necessary. This isn't the same

thing at all. This comes under the umbrella of letting someone help you.'

'Can I make you dinner, then?' She couldn't offer nothing in return for his generosity. 'Tomorrow night, as we'll still be here?'

'I wouldn't say no to that.' He smiled, and that was enough to make Ella think maybe she should stay for one more night.

CHAPTER SIX

LUKE STEPPED OUT of his house and headed for the cottage, followed by Maisie. He wasn't doing a very good job of keeping his distance, he realised. That strategy was failing dismally. He was unable to keep away. He felt himself drowning in the depths of Ella's dark eyes whenever she looked at him, captivated by her beauty and in awe of her strength. He knew she felt vulnerable but he saw her determination, her strength, her courage.

And so, once again, he found himself on her doorstep, unable to keep away. He had a small gift in one hand, a hostess gift. He'd deliberated if he should take one and what it should be. Ella was the hostess but it was his house. But the manners his parents had instilled in him wouldn't let him turn up empty handed. He could have taken flowers but she had a garden full of flowers at the cottage and would a bunch of flowers have given the wrong message?

What was the right one? What message was he trying to impart? What was their relationship? Landlord and tenant? Friends? She wasn't paying rent. And she wasn't a friend. Not yet.

He had settled on a box of shortbread, baked by Penny. Everyone loved Pen's baking.

Ella's hands shook as she took the pasta bake out of the oven and put it on top of the stove. She was equal parts excited and nervous. She was being ridiculous, she chided herself as she closed the oven door and straightened up. Luke was coming to dinner with her and Liv. That was all. It wasn't a date. It was a convenience for him and a thank you, a return favour, from her. There was no reason for her sense of anticipation.

Meeting someone she was attracted to when she'd embarked on her new path hadn't even crossed her mind. When she'd left Trent behind, she'd been determined to forge her own path, and survival had been her only goal. She hadn't had time to think about what her future would look like besides hoping she and Liv would have somewhere safe to live and she would have a job.

Meeting Luke was unexpected but she knew she had to put her feelings to one side. She had moved on physically and emotionally from Trent but she didn't trust herself to make good decisions with relationships. She knew Luke was a good man but that didn't mean he would be good for her. She'd made mistakes in the past and she had other priorities, bigger priorities, than getting involved in another relationship—even assuming Luke was attracted to her. And why would he be? She was a single mother with nothing to her name—no qualifications, no money, not even any possessions. It was her and Liv against the world. Who would want to take them on?

She would give Luke dinner as a thank you for his help and then they'd be gone, following her own path. Just her and Liv. As much as she liked the fantasy of a different life, she knew it wasn't likely to be her reality. Her luck was already tenuous; surely it wouldn't stretch to that she thought as she put any romantic notions aside and checked the table. Bowls, cutlery, a jug of water, glasses and paper napkins had been set out.

She'd placed a vase of flowers picked from the cottage garden in the centre of the table, but she reached for it now, removing it. Flowers were unnecessary. She carried them up to the bedroom and put them on the dresser, out of sight, before checking the time—again. She'd invited Luke for six-thirty.

Liv was lying on the floor drawing and she jumped up and ran to the door when they heard a knock. She opened it to let Luke and Maisie in.

Liv wrapped her arms around Maisie, who was wagging her tail vigorously in greeting, despite having spent most of the day at the barn with Liv, while Luke handed Ella a container filled with shortbread.

'I brought you these,' he said.

The biscuits looked home-made. 'Did you make these?' she asked.

'I wish I could lay claim to them but Penny baked them.'

'Well, they look delicious, thank you.'

He looked delicious as well. He was wearing shorts and a T-shirt and smelt clean and fresh, as if he'd just stepped out of the shower.

'Can I get you a drink?' she asked, stepping away to put the shortbread on the kitchen bench, trying to put some distance between Luke and herself.

'Just water will be fine, thanks,' he replied, before turning to Liv. 'How have you been today, Liv?'

'Good,' Liv replied. 'I taught Maisie to shake hands.'

'Did you? Can you show me?'

'Sit, Maisie.' Liv waited for the dog to follow

her instructions before she held out her hand and moved it up and down in the air. 'Shake.'

Maisie lifted a front paw and Liv shook it gently. 'Clever girl!'

'That's well done, Liv,' Luke said as Ella passed him a glass of water. He winked at Ella. She knew Maisie had already mastered that trick before but she appreciated that Luke was giving Liv all the credit. She smiled back at him as her nerves dissipated. He was a generous man, a kind man, and she didn't need to be so tense.

Luke sat on the couch, nursing his water, and continued his conversation with Liv while Ella dressed the salad she'd made.

'Have you had a headache today, Liv?'

'No.'

'You can see properly?'

'Yes.'

'Your eyes aren't blurry?' Liv shook her head. 'And you haven't been dizzy at all?'

'No. Can I play outside with Maisie now?' Liv asked Ella, apparently tired of Luke's questions.

'We're about to eat. Go and wash your hands now; you can play with her after dinner.'

Liv went to the bathroom and Luke turned to Ella. 'Liv didn't have any trouble following instructions or paying attention today? No nausea, no pain?'

Ella shook her head. 'No. We had a quiet day. Liv seemed fine, normal. We did some cooking—made this pasta bake and a cake. And she helped as normal.'

'That's good news.'

Liv monopolised the conversation through dinner, which relieved some of Ella's nervousness, and by the time she went outside to play with Maisie Ella had relaxed. She was getting used to Luke's company and to the cottage. She was beginning to feel safer, if still not completely safe, but she was more comfortable, less afraid and less nervous. Almost as though things might be okay.

'So, you didn't get on the bus today?' Luke asked when they were alone at the table.

'No. And there's not another bus until next Thursday.'

'Is that right?'

'You knew!'

'Does that matter? My advice still stands. Liv didn't need to be travelling today.'

'But I need to get settled somewhere before Liv starts school.'

'What's wrong with here?'

Ella pondered the question. What was wrong with here? It wasn't where she had planned to be but did that matter? The town had some appeal.

It was peaceful, had plenty of country charm and the people seemed nice—present company in particular. But already people knew her business. The town was small. Too small for her.

'I had a larger town in mind,' she said. Somewhere with more opportunity. Somewhere she could have anonymity. But to say those things out loud would sound like harsh judgement to someone who had chosen to make a life here. Someone who might have always lived here. 'You said you've known Penny all your life. Did you grow up here?'

'I was born here, grew up here. I went away to university and now I'm back.'

'What brought you back?'

'My dad was the local doctor. He retired a couple of years ago now. He had early dementia, and as it progressed he couldn't continue to work, so I came back.'

'Had you always planned to come back?'

'Not really. But it got to the point where I felt I didn't really have a choice. I knew Dad's mind was failing. He'd been managing at work—it was automatic; learned behaviour over so many years—but then Sam found him wandering in the main street. Dad couldn't remember how to get home. And alarm bells started ringing about how he was coping at home on his own. Penny and I arranged for some home help but then it became clear that work was too much for him as well. Eventually he needed full-time care and he moved into the nursing home. I'm the only family he has so I felt I needed to stay in town. He was also the only doctor, so I took over the clinic. Penny had worked for my dad, so she stayed to help me.'

'So is that why you go to the nursing home so often? Your dad is there?'

'I try to visit him every day. Sometimes it's more. He can get quite agitated and, if the staff can't calm him down, they call me.'

'That's a lot to deal with on top of being the only doctor in town,' Ella said. 'Do you ever bring your dad back here?'

'I used to bring him home for a meal but it's become too confusing for him. This was my parents' property—it's where I grew up—and Dad expects to see Mum here. He's forgotten she died and there's no point explaining that to him over and over. He finds it distressing or thinks I'm lying to him and gets upset. It's better if I see him at the nursing home. That feels familiar to him now.'

'So that explains why you live in such a big house on your own. Isn't it lonely?' She knew she was fishing for information but she couldn't understand why Luke didn't appear to be in a relationship. What was wrong with him?

'I'm not home enough to get lonely. Staying here was a convenience. I didn't think it would become permanent.'

'You didn't want to take over your dad's practice?'

'It wasn't my long-term intention and it certainly wasn't my fiancée's plan.'

'Your fiancée?' Ella couldn't believe she was only hearing about a fiancée now. Where had Luke been hiding her? Did he have skeletons in his closet too? 'Where is she?'

'In Adelaide, I think. I should have said *ex*-fiancée. She was my fiancée then but not now.'

'How long ago were you engaged?'

'We broke up two years ago. I came back to look after Dad but Mikayla had just started a new job in Adelaide—she's a doctor too—so we figured we'd be able to make a long-distance relationship work for a while. We'd take it in turns to make the ninety-minute commute every weekend.'

'And then?'

'Then Mikayla started refusing to drive up on weekends. Not outright refusing, but she had plenty of reasons why she couldn't make it. To be fair, there were times where I couldn't get away either, because of the clinic or because of Dad. And, when I decided to take over the practice, I assumed Mikayla would join me but she wasn't interested. Turns out she wasn't interested in living in the country. She wasn't a fan of the house, the job, Pelican's Landing or, in the end, of me. This move was never meant to be permanent and she accused me of being selfish. She said I didn't prioritise her, and she was right. I let her down and she left because of it.'

'Couldn't you have got another doctor to take over the clinic?'

'I tried but getting doctors to move to the country is a constant battle and I couldn't in good conscience close the clinic. I couldn't let my dad or the community down. Mikayla and I possibly could have reached a compromise but, by that time, the writing was on the wall. Our differences when we were twenty-five had seemed minor, but at twenty-nine they started to multiply, so we called off the engagement.'

'You don't have any regrets?'

'Plenty. I wish I'd been more considerate. I wish I hadn't let her down but I don't regret not being married to her.'

'And is Pelican's Landing where you want to be?' She wondered if he still thought of it as a temporary move.

'For now. I'm a country boy at heart. But, if you're worried about me being lonely, you and Liv can keep me company on Saturday.'

He was smiling, he certainly didn't look unhappy with his lot.

'Doing what?' she asked.

'It's the district agricultural show. It's a big deal around here. Liv will enjoy it. You might too.'

Ella had taken care getting dressed. She wanted to create a good first impression. Luke was taking Liv and her to the local agricultural show and, even though she knew it wasn't a date, she knew Luke would know everyone there and she wanted to look nice. For her own confidence and for Luke too.

She'd picked out a floaty summer dress, loose-fitting with long sleeves and a flowing skirt, to hide her bruises. She hoped people would think that her style was bohemian. She'd tied her hair into a low ponytail, trying to counteract the heat of the day. She adjusted her ponytail to accommodate a hat and then grabbed her bag and helped Liv out of Luke's car.

It was early afternoon and streams of people were heading in and out of the show grounds. They stopped at the gate and Ella's stomach dropped when she saw the entry prices. It was going to cost her fifteen dollars just to get in. She had water bottles in her bag but she wished she'd thought to bring some snacks with her. She'd been so full of anticipation and Liv had been such a bundle of excitement that she hadn't really considered how much a day out could cost her. But there was no turning back now. She'd have to figure out how to save her pennies once they were inside.

'Two adults and a child, please.' Luke had his wallet out and was buying tickets without being asked.

'Thank you,' she said as he handed her two tickets. 'Is it okay if I pay you back later?' If she paid him back now, she'd have no money left for anything inside the show grounds, and she was also still paying Penny back the money she had lent her to go shopping.

'Don't...'

She knew Luke had been about to say 'don't worry' before he stopped himself, saying, 'Sure. I'm happy to pay for your tickets but, if you'd feel more comfortable paying me back, that's fine.'

'Thank you.' She appreciated his comment. It gave her back her independence. She didn't want to owe people favours, she wanted to stand on her own two feet, and his reply make her think she was being heard, that he was listening to her, and that was important.

'What would you like to see first?' he asked Liv as they walked through the gates. 'There's a sideshow alley, rides, food, animals, animal rides...'

'What animals?' Liv asked. 'Is it a zoo?'

'No. This is a show for the farmers and their families. The farmers win prizes for the best-looking cow and the prettiest chicken. You can look at the farm animals and you can hold baby chickens.'

'Can we do that first?' Liv asked, tugging on Ella's hand.

Ella looked at Luke.

'Of course, follow me,' he said.

Liv spent the next hour holding baby chicks—being amazed by the different types of chickens, some with feathery feet and crested heads—and bottle-feeding lambs. Luke chatted to Liv about the baby animals in the nursery, amazing Ella again with how good he was with children, with people. He didn't ignore her either. He took her hand and made her sit on a hay bale to hold chicks and, when Liv insisted he have a turn, he sat beside Ella, their thighs touching as they squeezed onto the hay bale.

Ella's instinctive reaction was to shift herself away to create more personal space, but she had no room to move, so she forced herself to relax. Luke's presence wasn't threatening; in fact, she could feel his body heat radiating through the thin cotton of her dress and she found it strangely reassuring. She felt slightly disappointed when he stood up after handing the chicks back to the attendant.

As they left the animal nursery, they walked past a pony-ride enclosure where families were lined up, waiting for rides.

'Mummy, look, it's Chloe.' Liv was pointing at a family standing at the back of the queue.

Ella was surprised. She hadn't expected to see anyone she recognised but Liv was right: it was Hayley and her children from the adventure playground, Chloe and Jack.

'You know the Perrys?' Luke asked.

'If you mean Hayley, then sort of,' Ella replied. 'Hayley drove Liv and me to your clinic after Liv's fall. I'm surprised Liv remembers Chloe. She doesn't remember falling off the flying fox or being taken to the medical clinic.'

'Concussion can affect memory in strange ways,' Luke said. 'Do you want to say hello?'

'Can I have a pony ride? Please, Mum?'

Ella let Luke and Liv take her over to the

queue, where Luke introduced her to Hayley's husband, Josh. Of course, Luke knew the family. By the time the introductions had been made, Ella had thanked Hayley once again for her help and Hayley had asked after Liv's recovery, they were at the front of the queue and Ella hadn't yet made up her mind as to whether or not Liv should ride.

'Is it safe for Liv?' she asked Luke. 'What if she falls off? She's just recovering from concussion as it is.'

'Liv can run faster than these ponies are walking,' Luke reassured her with a smile. 'And the ponies are guided and the kids are wearing helmets. She'll be fine.'

Ella relented, trusting Luke's professional opinion.

'Stand next to Liv,' Luke instructed once Liv was settled on her pony. 'I'll take a photo for you.' He snapped a couple of photos of them both before taking his leave. 'I have to head off to the cake pavilion—I'm judging the scones. You can meet me there if you like or text me later and I'll catch up with you.'

'You're judging the scones?' Ella asked, but of course he was. Was there anything Luke couldn't, or didn't, do in this town?

Ella and Liv spent an hour with Hayley and

her family, while Hayley tried to convince Ella of the merits of enrolling Liv in school in Pelican's Landing, before they met Luke again at the cake pavilion where Penny had won the prize for best scones.

'That seems a little bit like favouritism, if you ask me,' Ella teased.

'It's a blind tasting,' Luke argued, as he handed Ella and Liv a plate of assorted scones. 'Here, I've saved these for you.'

'Don't tell me you don't recognise the taste or consistency of Penny's scones! You must have been eating them all your life!'

'Shh, I don't want you to get me kicked off the judging panel,' Luke laughed. 'When else do I get to eat as much as I like, all for a good cause? Now, time for sideshow alley.'

Luke took them to the row of sideshow games, where Liv played a fishing game before Luke shot basketball hoops to win a black-and-white soft toy dog for her, which she promptly named Maisie.

'What would you like, Ella?' he asked.

'I don't need anything.' She laughed.

'Of course you do. You know the old showground saying: *every player wins a prize.*'

'In that case, I've always wanted one of those sparkly dolls on a stick.'

'Really?'

'Yes, but I don't need one.'

'I can't imagine anyone would ever *need* one of those.' Luke grinned. 'But your wish is my command.'

'No, don't be silly. It's a waste of money.'

'I'll win you one.'

'You don't have to do that. Besides, you still have to pay to play a game. It comes to the same thing.'

'Well, it's my money,' he said as he promptly handed his cash over in exchange for table-tennis balls, which he proceeded to feed into the moving clown heads, calculating carefully until he did, in fact, win her the doll as promised.

Luke pulled out of the show grounds and headed back towards Pelican's Landing. Ella's mind drifted as she looked out of the window and watched the crop fields and livestock paddocks give way to orchards and olive groves as they got nearer the river and the town.

Luke hit the brakes, jolting Ella back to the present. A car was parked on the dirt beside the road. The hazard lights were flashing and the driver's side door was open but Ella couldn't see anyone.

'What is it?' she asked as Luke parked behind the seemingly abandoned vehicle.

'I recognise the car. I'll just be a minute,' he said as he stepped out.

Ella saw him crouch down beside the car and she could just make out the figure of a person slumped at the wheel. Luke looked back at her and gestured towards her with a wave. She unbuckled her seat belt and opened her door.

'Ella, can you bring my medical bag from the boot?' he called to her.

She nodded, told Liv to wait in the car, grabbed the bag and ran to Luke. A heavily pregnant woman sat behind the wheel. She was covered in a sheen of sweat and her hands were wrapped tightly around the steering wheel, giving the impression she was hanging on for her life. She cried out in pain as Ella handed Luke the bag, and Ella didn't need a medical degree to recognise she was in labour.

CHAPTER SEVEN

ELLA STEPPED BACK, uncertain about what she should do. Why was this woman on her own? Should she offer to help or stay out of the way? She stood silently as Luke spoke to the woman.

'Jane, I'm going to help you into the back seat after the next contraction. I need to see how far along your labour is.' His voice was quiet and calm. If he was concerned about the situation, he was hiding it well. He turned to Ella. 'Can you help me support Jane? She's going to need both of us to move her.'

Ella nodded and stepped closer. She waited for Luke's instructions and together they wrapped their arms around Jane's waist and half-pulled, half-lifted her out of the driver's seat and settled her as much as possible in the back seat.

'Let me have a look to see what's going on.' Ella stood in the open door, trying to afford Jane some privacy. 'The baby's head is crowning.'

'What?' Jane exclaimed, her tone equal parts

fear and disbelief. Ella felt the same. 'The baby's coming now?'

'Yes,' Luke replied. 'But I can see the baby's head, which means he's up the right way. So that's good news.'

Ella wasn't sure she agreed with Luke's definition of good news. 'Are you going to deliver the baby here?' she asked Luke.

'I'll have to,' Luke said as he stood up. 'Jane told me her husband is meeting her at the hospital in Murray Bridge. He's called an ambulance to meet Jane on the road but unless it arrives in the next few minutes they're not going to get here in time. I'm going to need your help.'

'My help?' Ella's eyes were wide.

'Yes,' he said as he rifled through his medical bag. He passed her a packet containing surgical gloves. 'Can you open the packet so I can get the gloves out, please?' he asked as he took a bottle of hand sanitiser and liberally covered his hands before rubbing them vigorously. He pulled the gloves from the packet and slid his hands into them. 'There should be a pack with a sterile sheet in the bag too. Can you find that and slide it under Jane?'

Ella couldn't believe Luke was going to deliver a baby on the side of the road. It was not an ideal situation in anyone's imagination. The road wasn't busy but the location still felt very exposed and vulnerable. She opened a second sterile sheet and clipped it to the seat belt and the door of the car, fashioning a temporary screen in an attempt to offer Jane a little privacy.

'Ella, can you climb in behind Jane?' Luke asked. 'Help her sit up slightly and then support her. It will be easier for her to deliver in a semi-reclined position.'

Ella went round to the other side of the car and crawled in behind Jane. Over her shoulder she could see a contraction rippling under Jane's dress. 'It hurts!' Jane cried out in pain.

'So I keep hearing,' Luke said, 'But apparently you'll forget all about it the minute you hold your baby. Isn't that right, Ella?'

'Have you got children?' Jane asked, her sentence broken into words uttered between panting breaths.

'A daughter.' Ella could tell Luke wanted her to distract Jane and she did her best to keep the woman focused on her. 'And Luke's right. You remember that it hurts but you really don't remember how much.'

'I want to push!' Jane cried out.

'Not yet,' Luke cautioned.

'You're doing great,' Ella told her. 'Just breathe in and out with me. We'll count to ten.' She hoped that was long enough for Luke to do whatever he needed to or to get Jane through the next contraction.

'Okay, Jane, well done,' Luke said. 'You can push with the next contraction.'

Jane gripped Ella's hand as she bore down. Her grip was ferocious but Ella knew she wasn't aware of it. Over Jane's shoulder she could see Luke ease the baby's head out.

'Stop pushing now, Jane. Little breaths,' he said as Ella watched him feel for the cord and ease it over the baby's head.

'All right,' he said. 'Push again with the next contraction.'

The baby, a boy, came out in a slippery rush and Luke scooped him up. He rubbed him firmly and was rewarded with a loud cry.

'Congratulations, Jane. You have a son,' he said as Ella heard the wailing of an ambulance siren in the distance. She climbed out of the car, knowing Jane wouldn't notice her absence now that she had a baby to hold, and flagged the ambulance down.

She waited while Luke handed over the care of his patient to the paramedics and they transferred Jane and her son to the ambulance. As they drove off she looked at Jane's car, abandoned on the side of the road. 'What are we going to do about that?' she asked Luke.

'Jane and her husband live in Pelican's Landing. I said I'll drop it off to their house. But only if you're okay to drive my car and follow me back?'

Ella was a little shaky; adrenalin was coursing through her system and she could only imagine how Luke was feeling. But she knew she was okay to drive. She nodded. She could do this favour.

Ella followed Luke back to town, collecting him from Jane's house and driving him back to the barn. Liv had fallen asleep and Luke carried her up to the loft while Ella put the kettle on.

'Thank you for your help,' he said to Ella as he came back downstairs.

'I'm not sure that I did much. You seemed to have it under control. Do you deliver many babies?'

'No. Luckily most mums make it to hospital. And being on the roadside was a first for me.'

'Jane was lucky you were there. Is it strange for you, knowing everyone in town socially and also treating them?'

'I don't treat all of them. I can separate one from the other. Some people choose not to use me as their doctor. There are other options—

they can go to Murray Bridge—but I can be trusted not to break a confidence.'

She knew that about him already. He had many good qualities; discretion was but one.

'Can I ask your opinion on something?' she continued as she poured water from the kettle into their mugs.

'Sure.'

'Hayley invited Liv over for a play date with Chloe. She might ask me to stay for a cup of tea but, if she doesn't, do you think it would be okay to leave Liv there? It's in the afternoon but I don't know if Josh will be home. Would Liv be safe there?'

'Josh and Hayley are good people. Josh and I went to high school together. Most people are, but I'm happy to be your sounding board while you're in Pelican's Landing. But what will you do when you move to Queensland? You're going to have to trust your own instincts about people.'

Ella shook her head. 'My instincts haven't been all that great in the past; I'm not sure I can trust them. And I'm also wondering about whether I should make the next move. I'm thinking that this place is starting to grow on me. And I have a favour to ask. I know you said no when it was a short-term proposition, but I'm thinking about enrolling Liv in school here. If I did that, we'd need somewhere permanent to live. Would you reconsider renting the cottage to me?'

Luke didn't answer immediately and Ella could see from his expression that he was reluctant. 'Is there a reason you don't normally rent it out?'

'Not one that makes sense to most people.'

'But it's so charming. It seems a shame to just let it sit empty. Why was it renovated in the first place?'

'I did it up for my sister, Gemma. But she never lived in it.'

'Your sister?' He'd never mentioned a sister. She'd asked about siblings and he'd said there was no one else around. She'd assumed he meant no one else anywhere. 'I didn't know you had a sister. Where is she?'

'She died.'

'Oh, Luke, I'm sorry. Was it recently?' That would explain why the cottage had been sitting vacant but Luke was shaking his head.

Ella handed Luke his coffee and put a plate of Penny's shortbread on the kitchen table as Luke took a seat and started talking. 'She died seven years ago. I'd just turned twenty-four; I was in Adelaide, in my sixth year of medical school, when it happened. Gemma was only nineteen. She had always been rebellious, born with a wilful streak, and she and Dad had frequent personality clashes. Dad expected us to study hard, set goals and achieve them. I followed a straight road, Dad's path, because it suited me. I'm a rule follower, but that wasn't Gemma's path. Her path was meandering, definitely not straight, but Mum was her champion. She always said that if Dad gave Gemma time she'd come good, she'd find her way. But then Mum died when Gemma was in her final year of school and Gemma lost her ally and her way.

'She and Dad were hurting—we all were—but Gemma and Dad couldn't support each other. Dad didn't know how to get through to her. She scraped through her final year of school and moved out of home the moment it was over. She got mixed up with a bad crowd and moved to Murray Bridge.

'I spent a summer fixing up the barn, hoping that if I could provide her with an alternative place to live, showed her that we cared about her, wanted to help her, she'd move back here. I knew she wouldn't move back into the main house but I thought she could be safe here. But she refused to move.'

'Sometimes it's hard for people to get themselves out of a situation,' Ella said. She knew that all too well from her own experience. It was easy to make excuses, much easier than finding a way out.

'I know. That's why I was trying to help her. I wanted to take a year off uni. I thought if I was close by I'd eventually be able to persuade her to come home, but my father insisted I go back. I still regret that. I failed her. And I failed Mum. Gemma never got the time to come good.'

'People make mistakes, Luke. You can't blame yourself.'

'So I'm told, but I'm not convinced. Gemma wasn't listening to me but I wish there had been someone else who could have helped her. People said that Gemma made her own decisions, but she was being influenced by the wrong type of people, and it cost her her life.'

'What happened?'

'Her boyfriend was a heavy recreational drug user and he was driving the car high on drugs. Gemma was with him and he crashed the car. She died. He lived. And I lost my sister.'

'That must have been devastating.' Ella knew what it was like to lose people, but he'd lost his sister and his mother in a relatively short space of time. It would have been horrendous, and compounded by the fact that he felt responsible in a way for Gemma's death.

Luke gave a wry smile. 'It wasn't the easiest of times. I gave up on the cottage after that.'

'It's sat empty for seven years?'

Luke nodded. 'I ignored it for the next six years. The cottage was meant as a refuge for Gemma, and I couldn't get my head around the fact that Gemma wasn't going to use it, so I just let it sit there. I was living in Adelaide; it was easy to ignore it. People suggested I rent it out but it seemed wrong to make a profit from something that was supposed to save my sister but ultimately failed.

'But the recent floods made me think of an alternative option. I have been considering using it as a refuge for locals in need of a place to stay. I thought that letting people stay for free would perhaps be a way to make sense of everything that had happened, but I was still finding it hard to let go of the idea that this was meant to be for Gemma. It was an emotional sticking point. I knew the physical act of letting the cottage out shouldn't be that difficult and what should be, in theory, a small gesture from me could be a much bigger deal to someone else. Penny says I couldn't have saved Gemma—she says I can't save everyone—but I didn't want to stop trying. And maybe letting someone in need use the cottage would help me to let go of my guilt over Gemma.'

'Is that what you were doing when you said I could stay? Were you trying to save me?'

'I'm not sure. Maybe, initially. But then I realised you didn't really need saving, you just needed time to breathe, time to process what had happened to you. I knew you'd figure out what you wanted to do next if you just had time to stop, recover and recuperate.

'I wasn't sure how it would go, having you in the cottage. I wasn't sure how I would feel. And I wasn't sure you'd accept the offer. I actually thought you might say no, that you might feel uncomfortable about staying so close to a stranger. I decided to let you take the decision out of my hands. You reminded me of Gemma in the beginning. You seemed fragile, in need of help, but I was mistaken. You're stronger than she was. You've got yourself out of a difficult situation. But I'm glad now that you're here. I'm glad the cottage has helped you, and you're welcome to use it for as long as you like.'

'Thank you. But I'll only stay if you let me pay rent. Even if you don't need the money, or it's an insignificant amount, I will feel better. I don't need charity. I don't want it. I'm wary of offers that are presented in neat little packages tied up with string. It's not what's in the package that bothers me. It's the strings.'

Luke nodded. 'Okay. I'll come back to you with a price.'

'Thank you.'

'Who wants another marshmallow?'

Luke had taken Liv, Jack and Chloe to find the perfect sticks for toasting marshmallows. He'd made a campfire and Hayley, Josh, Penny and Sam had joined Luke, Ella and Liv for a barbeque dinner to celebrate Liv's fifth birthday. They were sitting on Luke's front lawn, surrounding a fire pit which was set back from the river near a stand of gum trees. The pit was surrounded by cut tree trunks which the girls and Jack were sitting on to toast their marshmallows.

Ella had been touched by Luke's offer to host a party for Liv and she was trying not to be too disappointed that no one knew it was her birthday as well. She hadn't said anything; she didn't want a fuss and she'd become accustomed to giving her day over to Liv. But seeing the fuss everyone was making of her daughter—when it was usually all up to her—made her a tiny bit jealous that no one was making a fuss over her too.

'I hope you're leaving room for cake,' Penny

said as the children devoured yet another marshmallow and Penny emerged from Luke's house
carrying a large chocolate cake which she had
decorated like a farm yard with some figures
from a play set: chickens, a little girl and a
sheepdog like Maisie.

'Cake! Cake!' The children jumped up, aban-
doning their marshmallow sticks, to gather
around Penny while everyone sang *Happy Birthday* to Liv. Luke had been boiling a billy can
on the camp fire and he made tea and coffee to
have with the cake.

'Ella, have you had any luck finding a replacement car yet?' Sam asked as he tucked into a
sizeable piece of cake.

'No.' Ella shook her head. 'There is absolutely nothing suitable in my price range anywhere near here and I can't look further afield
as I've got no way of getting to the car yards to
inspect anything.'

'My nephew in Adelaide is selling his car. It
was my sister-in-law's first, so we know the history. It's a small four-wheel drive—I thought it
might be a good option for you. He's happy for
you to take a look at it before he advertises it.'

'Is it in Adelaide?'

Sam nodded. 'He's in the Adelaide Hills,
about fifteen minutes out of the city.'

'Tell him thank you, but how would I get there? Is there a bus from here that would stop in the hills?'

'Do you think he'd be happy to hold on to it until next weekend?' Luke asked Sam. 'I've got a meeting in the city on Saturday afternoon,' he said, looking at Ella. 'You could come with me and we can look at the car on the way.'

'I hate to sound ungrateful, but what would Liv and I do while you're at your meeting?'

'You could look around the city. My meeting won't be longer than two hours.'

'Or Liv could come to us for the afternoon, if you prefer, rather than dragging her to the city,' Hayley offered. 'We'd be happy to have her.'

'I'll message my nephew and let everyone know,' Sam said. 'That sounds like a good plan.'

Ella wasn't sure what the plan was, exactly. As with most things in Pelican's Landing, the locals made swift decisions and sorted things out with little debate. She wasn't sure if she liked the idea of not having a say. But the idea of spending a day with Luke alone had its merits.

Once everyone had finished eating cake, Hayley and Josh packed up their kids and headed home. Ella took Liv to the cottage to watch her brush her teeth before she hopped into bed. She came back to the fire to find Penny and Sam preparing to leave.

'You're going?'

'I'm afraid so,' Penny said. 'Sam is working tomorrow.'

'Thank you for celebrating with us,' Ella said. 'Liv had a fabulous day.' She was feeling quite emotional as she hugged Penny and Sam good-bye. It felt strange but good to be able to do that. She would never have been able to do that a couple of weeks ago. She was beginning to feel safe and comfortable surrounded by these good people, none of whom felt like strangers any more. They felt like friends.

As Sam and Penny drove away, Luke smiled at Ella.

'What are you smiling at?' she asked.

'You. I'm just thinking about how much you've changed in the past few weeks.'

'In what way?'

'You were so prickly, defensive.' He held up his hands and laughed as she opened her mouth to explain why. 'I get it, you had good reasons—your caution was perfectly understandable—but you've slowly relaxed your boundaries, dropped your guard. You're letting people in. And that's a good thing. Could you imagine, just two weeks ago, that you'd be hugging Penny and Sam? Or that you'd let Liv go on an unsupervised play date?'

Ella shook her head, amazed that Luke's train of thought echoed hers. 'No, I couldn't. I was just thinking how lucky Liv and I were to be stranded here. I feel like we're healing. It's been good for us. You and Penny and Hayley have been good *to* us, and I don't know how I can ever repay the favours.'

'We don't expect to be repaid. We're all happy to support you. It makes people feel good to help others. Seeing you enjoying life and smiling again is reward enough.'

'I know I've found it difficult to accept help, and I've probably sounded ungrateful, but I really do appreciate everything you've done and tonight you've really gone above and beyond, so thank you.'

'It's been my pleasure. And, now that we have the camp fire to ourselves, will you stay and have another coffee with me? It's only early.'

Ella smiled. 'I'd like that.'

'Grab a seat. I'll refill the billy and be back in a minute.'

He returned a few moments later carrying the billy in one hand and a small bag in another. He put the bag on the ground and the billy on the fire and sat down on the log beside her. Their thighs were almost touching and Ella found herself wanting to move a fraction closer so they would, in fact, be in contact.

Luke picked up the bag and handed it to her. 'Happy birthday.'

Ella looked at him with a confused expression as she took the gift. 'How did you know?'

'You filled in a form at the clinic. Your details were on there. Penny pointed out to me that your birthday is the same day as Liv's but we figured, seeing as you didn't mention it, you must want to keep it low key. But a birthday has to be acknowledged.'

'You didn't need to give me something. Having the party for Liv was enough.'

'The party was for Liv. This is for you.'

'Thank you,' Ella said as opened the bag, slightly overwhelmed that he had gone to this effort for her. Inside the bag was a gift-wrapped parcel, which she opened to reveal a photo frame. She turned it over. Luke had put a picture into the frame—it was the photo of her with Liv, the one Luke had taken at the show when Liv was on the pony. Ella was standing beside her, smiling directly at the camera, smiling at Luke. She barely recognised herself; she looked happy and relaxed.

'Thank you. I love it,' she said as, without thinking, she leant over and kissed his cheek.

'I'm glad you like it,' he replied as the billy started to boil on the fire. But Luke ignored it, choosing instead to reach out and hold her hand. He lifted it to his lips and kissed the back of her fingers. His lips were soft and warm. He lowered her hand into her lap before he lifted his hand slowly and stroked her cheek with his thumb.

Ella didn't move.

She didn't flinch.

She didn't pull back.

She knew it had become a muscle memory, an involuntary reflex, to retreat from contact but, if she'd learnt one thing over the past few weeks, it was that she could trust Luke not to hurt her. He'd been nothing but gentle and compassionate. Her world was gradually becoming what she'd hoped. Safe. Happy. And she had a lot to thank Luke for.

She knew she was safe from harm with him and it was a wonderful feeling. She closed her eyes as his thumb traced the line of her jaw and ran over her lips.

'Ella?' His voice was deep and soft.

She opened her eyes. The camp fire was dying down but there was enough light to see his features clearly. His blue eyes were dark, intense. 'Yes?'

'I would really like to kiss you.'

He'd asked for her permission. Ella's heart pounded in her chest and her breath caught in her throat. Unable to speak, she simply nodded.

'It would mean you'd have to find yourself another doctor,' he clarified.

'That's a sacrifice I'm prepared to make,' she replied with a smile.

Luke moved closer and she met him halfway, closing her eyes as his lips touched hers. She parted her lips, welcoming his tongue into her mouth, letting him explore her and taste her as she tasted him.

She opened her eyes to find him watching her. His gaze was unwavering and she could see desire in the dark depths of his eyes. She felt her temperature rise as a flush stole over her cheeks and anticipation burned bright inside her. She couldn't breathe; his gaze was so intense, it felt as if the air lacked oxygen, as if it was being burnt up in his gaze. She parted her lips to take a breath. Her lips were dry so she licked them with the tip of her tongue.

Luke groaned, giving in to his desire, giving in to hers. He wrapped one arm around her back, pulled her to him and kissed her hard.

He tasted of chocolate and coffee, of happiness and dreams. She waited for her nerves to raise the alarm, to ask her what she thought she was doing, but the anxiety didn't come, the alarm didn't sound. She wanted this; she needed this. There was no fear. She felt safe. She felt beautiful.

She could feel her desire building. She could feel herself falling into him. But she couldn't do it. She put a hand on his chest and Luke immediately stopped. Her lips felt cold and lonely but she had to stay strong.

'I can't do this,' she said. 'Not now. Not here.'

'But you're not saying never?'

Ella shook her head. The more time she spent with him, the more she liked him. She wished she was confident·enough to tell him just how much, but she had no idea how he'd react to that.

She couldn't deny she was attracted to him—she had been since the day she'd met him, although she'd spent countless hours trying to talk herself out of it—but he was out of her league. Successful, educated, well-respected.

But, as much as she would like to, she couldn't throw caution to the wind. Her judgement had let her down before. While at this moment this felt right, it felt special and magical, if she started something she didn't know if she would be able to stop it.

Liv was in the bed in the cottage. Ella couldn't take Luke there and she couldn't go with him to the main house and leave Liv alone, unprotected. At least by the camp fire she had a clear view of the door to the cottage. She would hear if Liv needed her. She would see her if she came outside. She had to stay on guard. She couldn't get distracted by Luke. She couldn't follow her desire. She couldn't forget her priorities, and her priority was Liv.

She didn't need any complication in her life. And men always complicated things.

CHAPTER EIGHT

LUKE'S LITTLE BOAT was tied to the jetty in front of his house. The river had peaked a couple of weeks ago and was almost back to pre-flood levels. It wasn't safe enough to water-ski on yet but Luke had said it was safe enough for a sightseeing excursion.

He stepped into the dinghy and handed out life jackets. He had a cooler box, a picnic basket, a blanket and beach towels sitting on the edge of the jetty and he stowed them in the dinghy while Ella and Liv put their jackets on.

Maisie jumped in and stood on the bow. Luke lifted Liv into the boat and then reached out a hand for Ella. His gesture reminded her of the day he had come to their rescue, but today she didn't hesitate. She took his hand as he helped her into the boat.

'Are we going swimming?' Liv asked.

'It's not safe enough to swim in the river yet. The current is still strong and there's a lot of debris floating in the water, but there's a little lagoon not far from here which we can check out,' Luke replied.

Ella looked around. There was no breeze and the surface of the river was flat and calm. Clouds overhead were reflected in the water and it mirrored the cliff face too. It looked beautiful. It looked peaceful, safe. But she understood that things were not always as they seemed. A calm exterior could hide all sorts of disturbing things.

Luke steered the dinghy through a narrow channel into a lagoon, past tall reeds and under low hanging branches, where he pulled into a small sandy beach.

'Will this be safe?' Ella asked as Luke jumped out of the boat and secured it to a tree. The water was murky and there was no way of seeing how deep it was or what lay beneath the surface.

'The water isn't flowing so quickly through here. There are no whirlpools or strong currents, so as long as there are no submerged logs or trees it'll be safe,' Luke said. 'But I'll go in first just to check it out.'

Ella and Liv waited on the bank as Luke stripped off. He removed his life jacket and then his shirt until all he was wearing was a pair of shorts. Ella let her gaze run over him. His shoulders were broad, his stomach flat, his arms muscular. For a man who seemed to always be at work, he was in good shape—very good shape.

Luke waded into the water, followed by Maisie.

Feeling self-conscious, Ella waited until his back was turned before she stripped off. She didn't have a bathing suit but took off her shirt to reveal a cotton camisole. She put her life jacket back on, fastening it above her shorts, and waded into the water with Liv when Luke gave them the all-clear.

The mud of the riverbed squelched under her feet. The water and the mud felt soft against her skin, not abrasive like beach sand and salt water, but she was reluctant to put her face into the river. She didn't like being unable to see the bottom, a fact that wasn't bothering Liv. Her daughter was a confident swimmer, having grown up on the coast, on the beach, but the life jacket was cumbersome, making things awkward. Liv was floating on her back and kicking her legs, swimming in and out from the shore with Maisie by her side.

Ella floated in the water, kept buoyant by her life jacket. Luke stood beside her. He wasn't wearing a life jacket but he was tall enough that his feet touched the ground.

The slight current started to pull her away

from his side. Luke held onto the strap at the back of her jacket and pulled her back to him. He was gentle, not rough, and she knew if she felt uncomfortable she'd be able to propel herself away and he'd let her go. But she liked being close to him. He felt dependable. He'd only shown her kindness, respect and consideration so far. He was handsome, smart and well-liked in the community—the sort of man who would make a good partner.

But that was a dangerous train of thought. Could she imagine settling down here? Despite the kiss she and Luke had shared, her intention was still to leave Pelican's Landing but, the more time that passed, the less she thought about it. Leaving was now an idea rather than a firm commitment.

Was she making a mistake? Was she letting desire turn her head, influence her decision? Was she imagining they could have something more than a platonic relationship? Despite the kiss, she wasn't sure she could even say they had a friendship—not yet. But she sensed they were on the edge of a precipice. The question was, how dangerous was the precipice—how high? If she stepped over the edge, would it all end in disaster?

She needed to keep her wits about her, she decided as she got out of the water. Getting caught up with Luke was sure to complicate things. She stripped off her life jacket, suddenly aware that her now-wet outfit was quite revealing. She stayed wrapped in her towel as she started to unpack the picnic Luke had prepared.

Luke took a rug from the boat and spread it out on the sand and Ella arranged fruit, cheese, cordial, water and ham sandwiches on the centre of the rug.

'What's it like to be five, Liv?' Luke asked.

'Good. How old is Maisie?' Liv wanted to know. She had a sandwich in one hand and was throwing a stick for Maisie with the other. The dog had endless energy and was happy to retrieve the stick from the water time after time.

'Four. But in dog years she's only a little bit older than your mum,' he teased.

'Hey!' Ella protested in mock offence. Luke winked at her and Ella melted.

He lay on his back on the rug, propped up on his elbows, keeping one eye on Liv, who had returned to the water with Maisie. Ella sat cross-legged next to him. She had ditched her towel and they sat close, almost touching.

'Ella, about next weekend, when we go to look at Sam's nephew's car—are you going to leave Liv here with Hayley for the day?'

'I think so, if she really is happy to have her. I thought if she came with us I could take her to the zoo or the beach while you're at your meeting, but if the car isn't suitable I might have to spend that time looking at other second-hand cars. That's not going to be much fun for Liv. And dragging her around car yards won't be much fun for me either.'

'In that case, I have a suggestion to make. I was thinking along the same lines. The price of the car is in your budget but there's nothing to say the car will be any good. My meeting isn't until the afternoon, but if we stay in Adelaide overnight we can look at other cars on Sunday before we come back, if we need to. Then it's just a case of whether you want to bring Liv with you or not. Hayley might be happy to have her for a sleepover. Or, if not Hayley, then Penny.'

'Where would we stay?'

'There's a hotel in the heart of the city not far from my meeting. I could book us two rooms there.'

'I appreciate the thought, but I don't think my budget would stretch to a city hotel.'

'I'm attending a board meeting. My accommodation gets paid for.'

'That's one room.'

'I'm happy to give you that room and book another one for myself.'

'Really?'

'Yes. And, just to be clear, it's a favour without strings. I remember, you're wary of strings. Think about it and let me know what you decide.'

A night in the city—just Luke and her. Was this the precipice? If she took up the offer, would the step prove to be too big for her? It felt huge, but was it really?

He wasn't asking her to make any promises. It was just a trip to the city; it didn't have to be anything more. Maybe he didn't intend it to be anything more but she knew she wanted to find out. She didn't feel comfortable pursuing anything in this small country town where everyone knew everyone else and their business. Perhaps in the city, if it felt right, they could explore this attraction.

Perhaps.

'I think you've got a good buy with that car,' Luke said as they turned off the highway and headed to the city.

'I really appreciate your help. I wouldn't have known what to look for,' she said. The best part about it, other than giving her back her independence, was the price. It had cost less than the insurance pay-out, leaving her with some extra money in the bank.

'What time did you organise to collect it tomorrow?'

'Around midday. We can have a late breakfast before we head off.'

Luke had determined there was no need to drive two cars into the city, so they would collect the car on their way back to Pelican's Landing. Ella could see the city skyline up ahead as Luke drove through the parklands that surrounded the CBD but she was surprised to see dozens of large tents, a Ferris wheel and several amusement rides set up in the park.

'What's all this?' she asked.

'The Adelaide Fringe Festival is on. It's an arts festival, a big one. Everything from cabaret shows, burlesque, magic, comedy, acrobatics, music and dance to visual arts. There are hundreds of artists and thousands of shows—it's a month-long party, basically. I thought we could wander through the gardens after I finish today, grab something to eat and go to see a show. What do you think?'

'It sounds like fun.' She had decided she would go with the flow for the weekend. No plans, no expectations. Hayley had Liv and Ella had nothing she needed to do, no one who needed anything from her. She could do as she pleased for twenty-four hours.

Luke pulled off the street into the driveway of the hotel, a few streets from the parklands. He handed his keys to the valet as a porter came to collect their bags.

'This looks a bit smart,' Ella said, meaning 'expensive'. Her brow furrowed as she wondered how much her room had cost. How much Luke had paid on her behalf.

'Ella, it's my treat,' Luke said as they approached the reception desk. 'The board has paid for my room and I'm happy to pay for yours. I can afford it; I don't have a lot to spend my money on. No strings, remember?'

Ella nodded as they stepped into the lift. Arriving upstairs, Luke swiped the card to unlock a door and held it open for her. 'This is your room—I'm next door.'

Her room had a view to the east, over the parklands with the hills in the distance. 'There's a Fringe guide on the table, if you want to look through it for a show that appeals to you. Will you be okay by yourself for the afternoon? I should be finished around five.'

'I'll be fine.' She smiled. 'I'm looking forward to having some time to myself.'

'Ouch! I thought you enjoyed my company.'

'I've been pretending, to make sure you let me stay in the cottage,' she teased. 'I do enjoy your company but I will be quite okay on my own for a few hours. I'll window-shop on Rundle Street and then lie by the pool.'

'That sounds tempting—the lying by the pool part, not the shopping. I'll see you later, then.'

Ella switched off the hairdryer and slipped her new sundress over her head. She had window-shopped along Rundle Street before using some of the money she had saved on the car to buy herself a cotton sundress and a bikini from a discount department store at end of the mall. It felt decadent to have new clothes but she refused to feel guilty about spending the money. She'd paid the insurance premium on her car and the money was hers to spend as she wished.

She'd bought Liv a present and she planned to use some of the remaining funds to pay for Luke's dinner. She had also bought herself a novel and had sat by the pool for an hour, reading. It was the first time in five years that she had had time to sit and relax without anyone making any demands of her.

She brushed her hair and used the hotel moisturiser on her skin. Her bruises had disappeared over the past four weeks and, for the first time in months, her skin was unmarked and she was able to wear a sleeveless summer dress in public. She had a slight tan from tending to Luke's garden beds, which had helped to camouflage the bruises as they had gradually faded. She applied a light lipstick and pulled her hair back into a ponytail; the day was still too hot to leave it loose.

She adjusted the straps on her dress, wondering if the emerald-green shade was a little too bright, a little attention-seeking, but the colour had seemed cheerful and had suited her mood. She felt reinvented, and it had been a while since she had felt so optimistic. Her new car represented freedom and independence. Wandering the streets of Adelaide alone, where nobody had recognised her or knew her business, had been cathartic. In Pelican's Landing, her secrets had been exposed to Luke and Penny and, even though they'd been nothing but supportive, it was naive to feel as though her past didn't shadow every step she took.

But now that she had a car it was time to think about her next move. She was pleased to have made the purchase, and very pleased to have her independence back, but she no longer had the excuse of a lack of transport keeping her in Pelican's Landing. It was time to make a decision about her next step—whether to stay or go. There were pros and cons to both options.

As she slid her feet into her sandals, she heard a knock on her door. Luke had changed into a pair of light cotton trousers and a blue polo shirt that enhanced the colour of his eyes. He was smiling at her and she found herself grinning in return. She was surprised at how easily he could make her smile.

'Hi. How was your meeting?'

'A little tedious, to be honest. I'm looking forward to some fresh air. Are you ready?'

Ella nodded and said, 'I'll just grab my bag.'

'Is that a new dress?' he asked as she stepped away to retrieve her bag.

'Yes.'

'That colour suits you.'

'Thank you.' Ella could feel a blush darken her cheeks and she was glad her back was turned. His comment was simple, an easy compliment that sounded sincere. She didn't think Luke was the type of man to give false compliments, but she'd been wrong about men before.

'Did you have a look at the Fringe guide? Was there anything that took your fancy?' Luke asked as they waited for the lift.

'It was a bit overwhelming, to be honest. There were far too many options. Would you mind if we just went for a walk among the tents and see if something jumps out at us?' She was quite happy just to wander and soak up the atmosphere.

'Of course.' Luke replied as they negotiated the crowds.

The streets had filled up as evening approached and Rundle Street had been closed to traffic. They wandered down to the parklands, mingling with the diverse crowd. Families, young couples and groups of friends sat at pavement tables or gathered around street performers.

Luke had booked a table at a Thai restaurant and, after dinner, he suggested dessert in the Garden of Unearthly Delights, which was part of the festival. They wandered down Rundle Street and into the parklands where the Garden sprawled under the enormous Moreton Bay fig trees, illuminated by lanterns. They wandered among the performance tents, soaking up the atmosphere, listening to the sound of hundreds of conversations competing with music from various shows and amusement rides, until they reached the far end of the garden, where a Ferris wheel loomed above them. A stall selling hot cinnamon doughnuts sat near the ticket office.

'How about doughnuts for dessert?' Luke asked.

'Can we take them on the Ferris wheel?' Ella replied. She wasn't one for high-speed amusement rides but she loved Ferris wheels.

They hopped onto the wheel just as the sun was setting. They chose west-facing seats, looking over the city and out to sea, where the sky was glowing red.

'Did you speak to Liv today?' Luke asked between bites of his doughnut.

'I spoke to Hayley this afternoon. Liv was far too busy to stop for a chat, but I could hear her in the background, and she sounded perfectly happy.' Hayley had offered to have Liv for the weekend, an arrangement that suited everyone.

'And you? Are you happy?' he asked.

She nodded. Right at that moment, she was happy. She had no cares. No worries. She felt light. Renewed. Refreshed. 'I am. I feel like I have turned a page and started a new chapter. I'm feeling positive about the future.'

'What does that look like for you?'

'I guess, now that I have a car, I'll get back onto Plan A,' she said.

'Queensland?'

She nodded.

'Soon?'

'I'm not sure exactly. I'm not in a huge hurry but I need to make the move at some point.'

'Why? Liv is happy at school. She seems settled.'

'She's five—she'll settle in somewhere else.' Ella knew she spoke the truth but she also knew that the sooner they moved, the easier it would be.

'Do you still want to move?'

She'd spent so many months dreaming of the move, planning the move, that she felt obliged to follow it through. And it still seemed like the most sensible option. She was happy in Pelican's Landing but her happiness wasn't going to pay the bills.

'I need to find a job. I think that will be easier to do in Queensland,' she said just as the Ferris wheel came to a stop with a jerk, throwing her against Luke. They were at the top of the wheel and the light breeze was swinging the carriage. Luke wrapped an arm around her shoulders to steady her. The sunset bathed his face in pink and orange but his eyes remained a brilliant blue.

'Is there any way I could convince you to change your mind?' he asked.

She smiled and tilted her face up to his. 'You can try.'

He pulled her closer and bent his head. She lifted her face to him and then his lips were on hers, warm and soft. She parted her lips as his pressure increased. He tasted sweet. He tasted of cinnamon sugar.

Luke had one hand resting on her bare arm, the other cupping her face. Her skin was on fire and she melted against him as her body responded to his touch. She was aware of nothing else except the sensation of being fully alive. She wanted for nothing except Luke. All her senses came to life and a line of fire spread from her stomach to her groin. She deepened the kiss, wanting to lose herself in him.

Her eyes flew open as the Ferris wheel started to move again, surprising her. Surprising them both.

Luke was studying her face, as if committing each of her features to memory. His fingers trailed down the side of her cheek, sending a shiver of desire through her. Her heart was racing in her chest and her breaths were shallow. That kiss might have been enough to make her consider changing her mind.

Luke took her hand as they stepped off the Ferris wheel when their carriage reached the bottom. They walked back to the hotel in silence. Ella was unsettled, her mind whirling. Jumbled thoughts rushed through her head so fast she didn't have time to formulate any words, let alone a full sentence.

The kiss had been wonderful, magical. She was attracted to Luke but she'd made mistakes with men before. She wasn't sure if she should get involved. Would she just complicate things? She wouldn't deny herself a chance to know Luke intimately if the opportunity presented itself, but she had vowed to be independent. Perhaps they could share one night; it didn't mean she had to change her plans.

'Would you like to come in?' she asked as they reached her door.

'Would you like me to?'

She nodded. She would take this as the opportunity she was after. He'd promised her the decision would be all hers—no strings. This was it.

Luke followed her into the room as she opened the door. As Ella stopped to slide her key card into the slot to turn on the lights, she was aware of how much space Luke took up in the entrance. He was broad, strong and tall and he towered over her, and she had a moment of nervousness in the semi-darkness until she flicked on the room lights.

As the room brightened her dark memories receded. If she was going to have any sort of future, in Pelican's Landing or anywhere else, she couldn't keep glancing over her shoulder looking for trouble or expecting the worst of people. Over the past few weeks, she and Luke had spent plenty of time together. They'd had many conversations. She knew she was safe with him. She had never had anyone listen to her or talk to her the way Luke did. She felt seen by him. Acknowledged.

And she couldn't deny she was attracted to him. She couldn't deny the desire he stirred in her. She didn't want to. She wanted him to make love to her. She wanted a new experience. She wanted newer, better memories to wipe out her painful past. Could she have this one night? One memory to take with her? She didn't expect anything more from him. Just one night was all she wanted.

But, now that they were in her room, she wasn't sure if she could take the lead. What did she do now? Should she reach for him? Tell him how she was feeling? She was unsure and her uncertainty made her take a step back just as he reached for her. She felt his fingers on the side of her face and she froze, waiting to see what he did next. But his touch was gentle.

Of course it was. This was Luke. She looked up and met his gaze. His eyes were a vivid blue, his expression serious. Everything about his body looked hard and intense but his touch was gentle, his fingers warm.

She put a hand on his chest. She wasn't sure if she was about to push him away or pull him closer. She waited for her nerves to raise the alarm, but the anxiety didn't come, the alarm didn't sound. Her heart was racing but not with fear or trepidation. Instead, she recognised the feeling as anticipation. It was a new sensation. She realised she wanted this, she needed this. There was no fear.

His left hand moved further down her back, cupping her bottom, pulling her hips in hard against him. She could feel his erection, separated from her only by a couple of layers of thin summer clothing. He was hard and long and now all she could think about was how he would feel inside her. She could feel the moisture between her thighs as she imagined him thrusting into her. Her knees wobbled and she clung to him.

His lips met hers, warm and soft. There was nothing hard about them, but his intentions were clear, spelt out in his touch as he pressed his lips against hers. Ella opened her mouth, desperate to taste him, to feel him, to experience him. She breathed out a sigh as he wrapped his arms around her, holding her to him. Her hands wound around the back of his neck. In another moment, there would be no turning back.

That was good—she didn't want to turn back. She felt safe in his arms. She felt beautiful. Desirable.

She reached one hand behind his head, holding him to her as she kissed him back. His tongue was warm in her mouth. His hands were warm on her skin. Every inch of her was on fire, consumed with desire. She felt his fingers on her bare arm, could feel them tracing a line up to her shoulder, across her collarbone to the sweet hollow at the base of her throat, felt his thumb dip into the little dimple. She couldn't breathe; she'd forgotten how.

She needed to breathe. She pulled away and he lifted his hands, releasing her from his touch. She almost begged him not to. She didn't want him to let her go.

'Are you okay?' he asked.

She nodded again, still unable to speak.

His dark gaze moved lower, over her chest. How could such blue eyes hold such heat, such intensity?

She held her breath, trying to stop the rise and fall of her breasts, but still her nipples peaked in response to his gaze burning through the thin fabric of her dress. She could feel the moisture between her legs as her body responded as his gaze devoured her. He wasn't laying a finger on her now and yet she felt ready to self-combust. A look, a glance, a smile was all it would take for her to melt under him.

'Do you want to stop?'

'No.' Her voice was breathless. 'I want you to make love to me.'

She didn't need to ask twice. With one arm, he scooped her up and held her against his chest, pressing her to him, and carried her to the bed.

CHAPTER NINE

LUKE GENTLY LOWERED her onto the bed and then eased himself over her and supported his weight on his elbows. She reached up and ran her hands over his biceps, feeling his strength, marvelling at the firmness within him. His body was hard but his touch was light.

His breath was coming fast now—she could hear it and feel it as it hit the bare skin of her shoulders and neck—but he didn't move. How could he hold himself so still? He was poised to move forward, to take this to the next level, but somehow he held his position. He was in no hurry. How could he be so calm when desire threatened to consume her? The waiting was exquisite agony. A delicious sense of anticipation battled with the desire to have him take her now, right now. She arched her hips up towards him, pushing herself against his groin, and was rewarded when she felt his matching desire, hard and firm, straining against his trousers.

She breathed out on a sigh as she let her knees fall open and wrapped her legs around him, pulling him closer, pulling him down against her. She heard him groan and he lowered his body until it covered the length of her. She wanted this. She wanted to feel his weight on her; she needed to know this was real.

Every cell of her body tingled in anticipation. She could feel each cell straining, reaching out to him. Her skin was on fire and every nerve-ending quivered with anticipation, alive with the possibilities of what was to come. Her expectations were almost painful, her reaction intense.

He reached for her, ending her suspense. His lips were on her ear lobe, soft and warm, his breath in her ear. He kissed her neck and then his lips covered hers. She melted into him and let him consume her. His fingers skimmed over her nipples, which grew hard and peaked. He swept the strap of her dress from her shoulder and exposed her left breast to the cool air. His thumb brushed over her nipple, teasing, tantalising. She cried out as a wave of desire washed over her and a bolt of heat scorched through her, sweeping from her nipple to her groin in a searing flash.

His lips left a trail of hot spots from her lips to her throat and collarbone, until finally he took her breast in his mouth, rolling his tongue over the taut flesh until Ella thought she might come then and there. But she didn't want it to end— not yet, maybe never. She wanted to feel him, to touch him, to arouse him too.

She pulled his shirt from his trousers and slid her hand under the fabric, running her hands over the warm skin of his chest. His body was firm under her fingertips. He cupped her breast in his hand and ran his thumb over her nipple, making her moan. She arched her back, offering herself to him, and he took one breast in his mouth again, sucking hard. Ella almost exploded in his arms.

She ran her index finger from his sternum down along the line separating his abdominal muscle, following the line of dark hair that led to his waist band. She concentrated on him, wanting to extend the pleasure, wanting to share the pleasure. She unbuckled his belt and snapped open the button on his trousers, unzipping his fly and pushing his trousers low on his hips. His erection strained against the fabric of his boxer shorts. She ran her hand over his shaft; it was strong and thick, and she felt it rise to meet her. Luke groaned and the sound of his arousal urged her on.

His hand ran up her thigh and the soft folds of

her dress fell away with his touch. His fingers met the elastic of her underwear and slid under the lace of her undies. Ella let her legs fall apart, opening herself to him, giving herself to him as his fingers slid inside her. She was slick and wet, throbbing. His thumb found her centre and she gasped as his touch took her to the edge.

But she didn't want it this way. She wanted to share the experience. She wanted all of him and she wanted him to have all of her. She let go of him and quickly pulled her dress over her head to lie naked before him. His dark eyes roamed over her body, setting her on fire with his gaze.

'You are so beautiful,' he murmured as he ran his hand over her belly and down between her thighs, seeking her warmth, sliding into her wetness.

She wanted to feel him inside her. She wanted them to be joined together. She lifted her hips and reached behind him, holding his hips, cupping his buttocks, pulling him close. Her knees were bent and she arched her back as she fitted him to her like pieces of a jigsaw. She thought she might melt on the spot as a burst of heat raced through her, flaring from her breasts to her groin. She sighed as he thrust into her, filling her, consuming her as they became one.

She gave herself to him and he claimed all of her.

'Oh, God, Luke,' she said as she clung to him, and she could hear the desire and need in her voice. Nothing else mattered.

There was nothing else.

She closed her eyes as stars burst behind her eyelids and sparks shot through her groin. She was panting now, unable to take deep breaths, as her body was focused on other sensations. She was close to a climax; she could feel it building, taking control.

Luke was drowning in Ella. He was losing control.

He felt her hand on his chest, felt it brush over one nipple and felt another surge of blood to his groin. He breathed her name and that was the last coherent thought he had. Her legs wrapped around his waist, pinning him to her. She pushed her hips against his and his resistance crumbled.

Her skin was soft, her eyes soulful, her body slim but not boyish. Her hips were rounded, her breasts full; he was completely mesmerised.

She tilted her hips and fitted him to her. He heard his own guttural moan as he thrust into her, filled her. He couldn't hold back, he couldn't resist, and when he heard her call his name it pushed him further.

There was nothing gentle in their love-making. It was fuelled by pure desire—desperate, all-consuming desire.

Everything else in his life was forgotten as Ella took over his senses. The world ceased to exist except for Ella. There was nothing else that mattered.

He wanted to go slowly; he wanted to savour the moment; he wanted time to commit it all to memory but he couldn't resist her. He couldn't fight it. He was only a man, a powerless man, and he could feel himself being swept away.

He thrust into her again. Up and down he moved, faster and faster, harder and stronger, and she met each thrust. She arched her back and held him close with her legs, opening herself to him, offering herself to him.

He buried himself deep inside her and, when he felt her shudder and come undone, he came with her. They climaxed together and, when they were completely spent, he gathered her to him, holding her close, reluctant to let her go as he savoured this next moment.

She had blown his mind. She was bold and confident. This was the Ella who had been hiding—the one he had suspected might be in there somewhere, the one who had been swamped by trauma and stress. He was finally piecing her together. Bit by bit, he was getting to know her and he was amazed by her strength, resilience and positivity.

He felt a drop of moisture on his naked shoulder and his heart missed a beat as he saw Ella wipe away a tear.

'Ella? Are you okay? Did I hurt you?'

He was horrified to think that he had upset her or, worse, hurt her; she needed tenderness, kindness and compassion.

But she hurriedly reassured him. She smiled as she looked at him and said, 'No. Not at all. These are happy tears. Emotional but in a good way. I didn't know sex could be like that.'

'Like what?'

'Amazing. Satisfying. I've never had a partner bring me to an orgasm before.'

'Never?'

She shook her head. 'I've only achieved that on my own. I don't think sex has ever been about me before.'

'What about before your ex? With Liv's father?'

'No. We were young. I don't think he really considered me at all. It was all over in a flash.

Her conception wasn't the beautiful experience I would have chosen.'

'We will have to see what we can do to change your experiences.'

'Tonight was enough.'

'Really? You don't want to do that again? I'm sure we will only improve with practice,' he said as he turned onto his side and gathered her in his arms.

'No strings, remember?' she said. 'And don't forget my Plan A.'

Her Plan A. She was moving to Queensland.

But, as he felt the weight of her in his embrace, as he looked at her face, something tugged at his heart and he felt something tug at his soul. 'What if you didn't have to go? What if you got a job in Pelican's Landing?'

What was he doing? The words were out of his mouth before he had time to think things through. They'd had great sex but that didn't have to mean anything more. It didn't have to *be* anything more. He wasn't ready for a commitment so what exactly was he proposing?

She frowned. 'What would I do?'

It was too late now. He was in over his head but he couldn't retract his suggestion. 'What were you planning on doing in Queensland?'

'Something in the hospitality sector, probably. I thought I could get a job in a hotel reception.'

'Is that what you'd like to do?'

'Not really. But it's something I have experience in.'

'What's your passion?'

'Numbers.'

'Numbers?'

Ella nodded. 'I was at university studying accountancy when I got pregnant with Liv. I was in second year but I never went back. I had a student job in a pub and I went from there to work in the yacht club.'

'Why don't you go back and finish your degree?'

'I haven't got the time or the money to go back to uni. I need to work, but I have been thinking about doing a bookkeeping course. Maybe even combining that with some work in the domestic violence space. Women almost always suffer financially as well as emotionally and physically in those situations. There must be a need for education or assistance around that.'

'If you could get a part-time job and study would you consider staying in Pelican's Landing?'

'Are you asking me to stay?'

'I'm asking you to consider it. Liv seems to be

settling well; it would be a shame to move her, and it's a good community. I think you could be happy there.' He didn't want to let her go but he was afraid to ask her to stay. Afraid he'd let her down.

Ella couldn't pinpoint exactly when she'd given in and decided to stay in Pelican's Landing.

Maybe she'd given in because she saw how happy and settled Liv was. Maybe she'd given in when she'd enrolled in an online bookkeeping course, or maybe it was when she'd found part-time work at the local pharmacy, thanks to Luke's contacts.

Or maybe it was because she wasn't ready to say goodbye to Pelican's Landing or to Luke. Not that she'd admitted to herself yet that the move might be permanent, and still wary of relationships she was reluctant to acknowledge that her feelings for Luke had played a part, but she was finding him addictive.

They weren't officially dating but there was no denying their relationship was progressing. They hadn't put any labels on it—she thought they were both afraid of having that discussion—but she was enjoying his company. It felt safe, and he was gentle and considerate, both in and out of bed.

They hadn't gone public yet, and even Liv was unaware of the fledgling relationship between her mother and Luke, although Penny and Hayley knew. Luke had convinced Ella to tell them and she had to admit that, without Penny's and Hayley's assistance, she and Luke would have very little time together. Last night had been a prime example. Liv had been at a sleepover at Chloe's house, giving Ella a precious night to spend in Luke's bed.

She lay on her side in his enormous bed, watching him as he slept. He was so beautiful—beautiful, gentle, kind and generous—and she was slowly learning to trust him. Slowly learning that letting him into her life didn't mean giving up her independence or her identity. Rather, with his kindness and compassion, she felt she was beginning to blossom into the person she was supposed to be.

At moments like this she wondered if she could, just for now, let desire rule her head and heart and allow herself one tiny glimpse of how life would be if it were perfect. What woman with red blood coursing through her veins would be able to resist temptation when it was presented as beautifully as this?

But every now and then she experienced a niggle of anxiety, a strange sense of foreboding.

Had she given in too easily? Had she sold out her dream of independence for a man she barely knew? A man who barely knew her? Sometimes she was afraid the answer was yes and her decision was going to turn out to be a bad one.

Luke opened his eyes and smiled when he found her watching him. The bed sheet was around her waist. She was naked, they both were, and she saw his blue eyes darken with desire as he took in her nakedness. She was amazed at how unselfconscious she felt as she returned his gaze.

He reached out and rested the palm of his hand against her ribs and she could feel the beat of her heart pulsing under his fingertips. He ran his fingers lightly over her nipple. It peaked and throbbed under his touch. She licked her lips and Luke groaned, and then his hand was on her face, cupping it with infinite gentleness and tipping her face down to his.

The moment his lips touched hers, Ella was no longer quite aware of where she was; all she knew was this moment should go on for ever. She was no longer sure where his body ended and hers started, couldn't have said whether she was standing or sitting. There was only the kiss. Nothing else. Only Luke's mouth on hers, touching, kissing, caressing, as if they'd been made for this moment. She sank deeper into his touch, his taste, all her senses trained on Luke and how he was making her feel. Every molecule was alive with his touch and her head was pounding with desire.

He ran a hand from her cheek to her shoulder and down her arm to her elbow, leaving a trail of fire in his wake. Then slowly, gently, he slid his fingers between her thighs. She parted her knees, letting her legs fall apart, granting him access to her soul. His fingers worked their magic, turning her insides into a pool of treacly deliciousness and compelling the blood to rush from her extremities to where it was really needed, leaving her toes strangely numb and her belly on fire. She arched her back as his fingers took her to the peak of ecstasy. Behind closed eyelids, all she could see were colours dancing to the thrum of her blood in her ears as she gasped and shuddered, climaxing while he watched her.

Satisfied and happy, she caught her breath and then sat up and straddled him. She put her hands on either side of his head as she let him guide himself inside her. She straightened up and traced her fingers across his chest where the morning sun touched his skin. His hands were on her hips, lifting her up and down, and she leant backwards, making sure she could take his whole length, riding him until he joined her in exquisite relief...

'Good morning.'

'It is a good morning,' she replied with a grin as she collapsed onto his chest. 'It's a beautiful morning.'

'What time do you need to collect Liv?'

'Not until ten.'

'Well, I'll let Maisie out and make us both a cup of tea, and then we might as well spend the next hour in bed. Unless you have other plans?

'I have absolutely zero plans.'

Ella lay back on the pillows as Luke got out of bed and padded naked out of the room. She watched him go with a smile on her face, enjoying this moment of complete bliss and satisfaction. This was a good moment. This life felt like a fantasy, a dream. Could it be real? She was having amazing sex with a gorgeous man, she had a job, Liv was happy in school and they were safe. It was the new start she had dreamed of but she still didn't dare to think it could be real.

Luke had told her she deserved this life. That she had been brave and strong and had made this happen. He tried to allay her fears, had told her not to over-think it, to enjoy it, but sometimes it was hard to let go of the anxiety.

Luke was smiling as he made the tea. His relationship with Ella was progressing slowly, their time together limited by Liv, but the slow pace had removed some of the pressure.

Ella was strong, resilient and determined to make her own way and his fears of letting her down were gradually dissipating in the face of her independence. She wasn't making any demands on him. She was busy, they both were, and he was just enjoying spending time with her when he got the chance. They hadn't put any labels on what they were doing and they'd made no promises, no commitments. If their relationship wasn't official it took the pressure off them both. It lifted the weight of expectation from his shoulders and removed some of Ella's doubts about her choices.

The only, somewhat ironic, concern he had was his own increasing reliance on Ella. Since his return to Pelican's Landing, he'd always had plenty to keep him occupied—his work, community events and his father—and he'd never felt lonely but now, the nights when Ella was not in his bed felt long and empty and his thoughts constantly turned to her. He had no idea if she planned to make Pelican's Landing her permanent home—they hadn't broached that subject—but as the days and nights passed he was beginning to wonder if they should have that conversation. Perhaps one day soon he'd find a way to raise the topic, he thought as he carried the tea into the bedroom.

Ella was sitting up in bed holding her phone, but his heart dropped like a stone when he saw her expression. Her face was pale, her brown eyes wide.

'What's happened? What's wrong?' he asked.

She looked up at him and her hand shook as she let her phone fall on the bed.

'My ex. He's back. He's looking for me.'

'I thought you said you had a new phone? A new number?'

'I do. This is an email.'

'You didn't change your email?'

Ella shook her head. 'I needed it for my government accounts. He can't track me through an email, can he?'

Luke wasn't sure. He didn't think so, but he'd never had to consider that question before. He crossed the room, put the tea cups on the bedside table and picked up Ella's phone. The email was still on the screen. He scanned the contents. The message was brief but the tone was menacing and threatening, promising he would find her. It was nasty and Luke could understand why Ella was shaken. If she replied, would there be any way of him tracking where it had come from?

'Don't reply,' he said. He couldn't imagine she would want to but it was better to make sure she didn't. It was better to be safe than sorry.

'What if he comes after me?'

'Does anyone know where you are?'

She shook her head.

How did people track someone down? Luke had no idea. Liv wasn't Trent's child, so he had no rights there, but joint assets would have to be disclosed, wouldn't they? 'Do you have any joint assets?' he asked. 'Did you have a joint bank account?'

'We did but I took my share of the money out and opened another one with a different bank before I left. I haven't used the joint account. Could he find me through my car?'

'The car that was swallowed by the river?'

Ella gave a half-smile. 'I can't believe I'd forgotten about that for a minute. It's one way to get my mind off my other problems.'

'Was the car in joint names? Is he on the insurance policy?'

'No.'

'So, the insurance company doesn't need to notify him, so that's a plus. Is this the first time he's tried to find out where you are?'

She nodded. 'He has been away for six weeks for work. He would have just got back to Geraldton and realised we weren't there.'

'I don't think he'll be able to find you.'

'But you said everyone in town will know I'm staying in your cottage.'

'Ella, he sent you an email, he doesn't know where you are. He'd have to track you to South Australia first and then to Pelican's Landing. It would be like finding a needle in a haystack.

'But can I make a suggestion that might help allay your fears? Why don't you speak to Sam? He'll have a better idea of what you should do in these circumstances. I'll call him and see if he can meet us at the station later today. We can pick up Liv and I'll look after her while you speak to Sam.'

'Can you call him now? The longer I wait, the more I'll worry.'

Ella was exhausted. She'd taken Luke's advice and had come to speak to Sam but having to recount all the details of her relationship with Trent had left her shaken and distressed. Going over the abuse had been almost as traumatic as the abuse itself.

And Sam's questions kept coming. 'Have you ever called the police for assistance? Made a complaint? Pressed charges?'

No. Why hadn't she? She'd left because he'd hit her in front of Liv. She hadn't want Liv to see that and she didn't want Liv to be in danger. But she'd never pressed charges. Never called the cops.

'Have you ever been to the doctor? Would a GP have any record of any injuries you sustained from Trent?'

Ella shook her head. 'Luke is the only doctor who has seen the bruises but that was when he stitched my leg up after the flood. That was weeks after the last incident and I wasn't consulting him about the violence.'

'Do you have any dated photos of any of the bruises?'

'Yes.' She nodded. 'I do have some on my email.' She'd taken some and emailed them to herself, knowing she couldn't leave them on her phone in case Trent saw them.

'That will help. I would suggest that you put an interim intervention order on him. That will prohibit him from contacting you or coming near you or Liv.'

'What evidence do I need?'

'This statement you've given me plus some photos will suffice initially. If he disputes the order, then the matter would go to court.'

EMILY FORBES

197

Ella paled at the thought of having to confront Trent in court.

'You wouldn't have to be there in person,' Sam reassured her.

'How long does it take to put an intervention order in place?'

'It is in place as soon as it is served—so, as soon as it is handed to Trent. All I need is his address details in Western Australia. I'll get someone there to deliver the order.'

Luke had collected Ella from the police station and taken Liv and her out for dinner. Neither of them had felt like thinking about cooking meals, and Luke had thought it would keep Ella occupied. But neither of them had counted on Sam calling with the news that the West Australian police hadn't been able to locate Trent. Sam had wanted to know if there was anywhere else Trent might be, any common haunts, but Ella had only been able to think of the local pub. She'd left dinner feeling queasy and nervous.

'Will you and Liv come and spend the night in the big house? Would you feel safer there?' Luke asked when they got home and Liv ran ahead of them to cuddle Maisie, who was waiting to greet them.

'Thanks, but I don't want to have to explain

why we'd be sleeping in your house to Liv. I don't want to tell her what's happening. We'll be okay in the cottage.'

'Well, in that case, why don't you get Liv to bed and I'll come back and sleep on the couch? I'd feel better if Maisie and I stayed here. Would that be all right? I'll be gone in the morning before Liv wakes up.'

Ella was trying to be brave, trying not to rely on Luke but his offer was too generous to refuse. She knew she would sleep better knowing Luke was there. 'Thank you, that would make me feel better.'

It had been days since she'd given Sam her statement and put the interim intervention order in place, and still Trent hadn't been served with it. Ella was on edge and she knew she would be until Sam came with good news.

She had picked Liv up from school and was preparing afternoon tea when she heard a car coming down the drive. It wasn't Luke's—she knew the sound of his car now—so she glanced out of the kitchen window to see who was approaching the property and her heart jumped as fear and disbelief gripped her.

Behind the wheel was a familiar but unwelcome face.

Trent, her ex, was heading for the cottage.

She clutched at the kitchen bench and took a deep breath, trying to slow her racing heart. What was he doing here? How had he found them?

She had no time to run.

And nowhere to run too.

Her mouth was dry as her eyes darted around the room, looking in vain for an escape. What could she possibly do to keep Liv and her safe? Did she have time to get Liv into her car? Even if she did, there was only one way out of the property, and she'd come face to face with Trent on the driveway. She knew he would park behind her car, blocking her in, and the path would lead him though the garden, directly to the cottage door.

The one door mocked her complacency from across the room. That sole exit point had bothered her from the get-go but she'd convinced herself she was safe. She'd been foolish, lulled into a false sense of security by the remoteness and slow pace of Pelican's Landing. She hadn't been able to imagine anyone looking for her here.

The wooden door was solid but would it be secure enough to keep him out? Oh, God, had she locked it? She ran to check it. She was sure she would have; it was still a force of habit, even if she'd started to feel safe.

She breathed out a sigh of relief as she saw the lock was set. Out of the corner of her eye she could see Trent's car heading towards Luke's house. He'd missed the turn-off to the cottage. How long did she have before he realised his mistake?

She quickly yanked the curtains across the windows overlooking the garden; perhaps she could pretend they weren't here. But he would eventually see her car parked out the front. He must have followed her here from town. Her car was going to give them away.

Liv was sitting at the kitchen table, pulling her lunch box and reading folder out of her school bag.

'Liv,' Ella said, fighting hard to keep her voice calm and steady as she returned to the kitchen bench. Fear made it wobble but she hoped Liv wouldn't notice. 'Can you go into the bathroom and wash your hands, please?' Her hands were trembling as she picked up Liv's cup and plate. She squeezed the cup hard, not wanting to spill the drink, and followed Liv into the bathroom. She heard the car stop and reverse. He must have gone past the fork in the driveway that led to the cottage. He would have seen her car. She heard the sound of his car reversing back before turning towards the cottage.

She needed to hurry.

'Liv, I need you to listen to me. Trent is here. He's driving up to the house now.'

Liv's eyes were wide.

'I need you to stay in here and lock the door. You can eat in there, but be very quiet, and do not come out until I knock on the door and tell you he's gone. Okay? Can you do that for me?'

She kissed her forehead and closed the door. She heard Trent's car stop out the front and the engine cut out. 'Lock it now, Liv.'

Her heart was hammering.

She went and stood in the kitchen, putting the kitchen table between her and the front door as she heard Trent's car door slam.

The knife she'd used to cut Liv's apple was in the sink. Should she grab it? Arm herself? Protect herself? But what if he took it off her and used it against her? She was frozen in place by indecision and fear.

Her bag was on the table. She grabbed her phone from it and opened her messages. Penny had been the last person to message her. She tapped the message and quickly typed:

Call the police. My ex is here.

She hit send just as she saw the door handle turn. Her heart was in her throat, her eyes wide with fear as she watched the handle turn and prayed the lock would hold.

'Ella, what the…' His next word was drowned out by the sound of a heavy crash against the door. 'I know you're in there. Let me in.'

Ella's throat was tight with fear. There was no way she could speak, no way she could answer him. She knew she needed to defend herself but she hadn't the slightest clue how to do that.

She had to keep him out. The door vibrated as Trent either kicked it or rammed it with his shoulder again.

Should she have locked herself in with Liv?

No; she couldn't risk him getting to Liv.

Should she go outside or wait here for the police? She was trapped in here, caged. Would she have more chance of escape if she was out in the open? But she couldn't risk leaving Liv in the house unguarded. She needed to keep Trent away from her.

Ella's heart was hammering. She had to stall Trent until the police came and she was about to call out when the lock splintered under Trent's force and the door flew open. Ella darted behind the kitchen table, needing to put something between her and Trent.

His eyes blazed with anger as he advanced towards her. 'You're mine, Ella. If you think you can run off, you're a stupid woman. I told you'd I'd find you.'

'Trent, we were just taking a trip. A holiday. That's all.' She needed him to think she'd been coming back.

'Don't lie to me! You've stolen my money and changed the bank accounts.'

'That was *my* money I took. Mine!'

He stepped towards her fast, and she wasn't quick enough to get away. She was angry and frightened and she wasn't paying enough attention. He lashed out with his right hand, back-handing her across her face, and she went flying.

Her left hand hit the tiled floor, breaking her fall before she crashed into the kitchen cupboards. Her head hit the cupboard and Ella saw stars. She could feel an egg form immediately on the back of her skull.

Trent took two steps towards her and, dazed, she struggled to her feet, afraid if she stayed on the floor that he would kick her. Her left forearm was hanging at her side and as she tried to bend her elbow she cried out in pain. She squeezed her left arm against her side and tried to dash past Trent. If she could make it out of the door, she'd have more room to run and she'd be able to lead him away from Liv.

She thought she'd made it past him until she felt herself being pulled off her feet. He'd grabbed her by her hair and she felt a chunk of it being ripped out by his hands. Her knees buckled as she tried to find her footing and Trent pulled her to her feet again, but this time his hands were around her throat.

She could feel him squeezing, and she tried desperately to claw his hands off her, but her left arm was useless and she was no match for him with only one hand.

She was running out of air.

She was crying in fear, desperation and pain. She knew she was using up her last gasps of precious air but she couldn't stop.

Trent's face was contorted with rage. She could see his lips moving, and she knew he was yelling at her, but she couldn't hear anything. Her senses were fading with her breath.

Black spots danced before her eyes…and then there was nothing.

CHAPTER TEN

LUKE TURNED INTO his drive and took the left fork to the cottage. He'd picked up some fresh peaches for Ella from a roadside stall on his way back from a home visit and thought he'd drop them off for Liv to have for an after-school snack before he returned to the clinic.

An unfamiliar car was parked behind Ella's four-wheel drive and he assumed Ella must have invited a friend of Liv's over for a play. Luckily, he'd bought a whole tray of peaches, he thought as he parked and lifted the tray from the back seat.

The door to the cottage was open but it was very quiet. He couldn't see or hear anyone. He stepped through the doorway and searched the room.

The tray of peaches hit the floor with a dull thud as he launched himself across the room. His legs propelled him forwards before his brain had properly registered what he was seeing.

A man was standing over Ella.

His hands were around her throat.

Luke's movements were a reflex, a preservation reflex. Not for his own sake, though—for Ella's.

Luke collided with the man, laying a rugby tackle on him and taking him by surprise. He let go of Ella and Luke was vaguely aware of her collapsing to the floor before he landed heavily on the kitchen table with Ella's assailant underneath him.

The table splintered under their weight and the man came up swinging. Luke had just enough time to register that this must be Trent, Ella's ex, before he felt Trent's fist smash into his face, just above his left eye. Luke shook his head, committing to the fight. All he could think of was that he had to keep Trent engaged. He had to keep him occupied, had to keep him focused on himself and away from Ella.

He landed a fist in Trent's stomach and was pleased to see Trent double over. His satisfaction was short-lived, though, as he copped a return blow to his abdomen before he felt Trent's knee slam into his thigh.

The fight wasn't pretty, fighting wasn't his style, but he had to protect Ella. He managed to land a couple more hits while taking a couple in return until suddenly the blows stopped coming. Trent's hands were covering his face and Luke could hear him coughing.

Luke turned and saw Sam standing beside him, holding a canister of pepper spray. All the fight went out of Trent as Sam handcuffed him and led him outside.

Luke hurried to Ella's side.

She was sitting on the floor, her knees pulled up against her chest, as if trying to make herself as small as possible, as inconspicuous as possible. She was leaning against the couch, her arms at her sides. Her face was pale but Luke could see angry red marks on her neck where Trent had choked her with his hands and he knew the marks would turn into bruises.

He crouched down beside her and wrapped his arms around her. She closed her eyes and let him hold her. He could feel her shaking. 'It's okay. You're safe. Are you all right?'

'Yes. No. I don't know.' Her voice was hoarse.

'Where's Liv?' Luke was concerned.

'She's in the bathroom. I need to tell her she can come out.' Ella started to get up.

'I'll get her.'

'No.' She held onto his arm and pulled herself to her feet with her right hand, wincing in pain. 'I told her not to come out until I came for her.'

'Are you hurt?'

'My arm.'

Ella's left arm was dangling at her side. She had her right hand pressed to her left upper arm, holding it against her body, but Luke could see her left elbow was misshapen and he knew immediately that it had been dislocated. He put his arm around her waist, letting her lean against him, supporting her. She was wobbly on her feet, pain and shock combining to make her unsteady.

A drop of moisture fell from Luke's brow. He wiped it away with the back of his hand while still holding onto Ella. His hand came away streaked with blood. Trent's fist must have split the skin above his eye. He pressed his fingers against the cut, trying to stem the blood, knowing Liv would be scared and not wanting to frighten her any further.

Ella knocked on the bathroom door. 'Liv, sweetheart, it's Mummy. Trent is gone, you can open the door now.'

Luke heard the key turn in the lock but Liv didn't emerge. Ella opened the door to reveal Liv, pressed against the wall between the basin and the toilet. She looked terrified.

Ella let go of Luke and hurried across the small room, her injuries forgotten in her haste to reach her traumatised daughter. He watched her gather Liv to her with her good arm, holding her close.

'It's okay, we're safe.'

'Where's Trent?'

'Sam has taken him away. He's putting him in the police car right now.'

Ella was talking quietly to Liv but from his position mere steps away Luke could hear every word. He wondered how often this scene had played out before Ella had found a way to escape.

Liv and Ella were both shaking, shivering, and he knew Ella must be in agony. He let her comfort Liv and then guided them to the couch. He used his body to try to block the view of the destruction—the room was littered with fragments of broken furniture and smashed crockery.

Luke took a moment to assess Ella's arm. It was definitely dislocated but, listening to her describe what had happened, he was concerned that she might have fractured it as well. Fortunately, the colour and sensation in her hand and fingers was normal, and so was her wrist pulse, so he hoped she had escaped any serious nerve damage, but she'd need an X-ray before he could safely reduce the dislocation.

Ella was quiet throughout his examination and Luke was worried about her.

Sam reappeared, carrying a first-aid kit. Luke knew that wasn't what he needed to take care of Ella. 'I need to take Ella to the clinic,' he said, one eye on the kit in Sam's hand. 'She's dislocated her elbow.'

'The kit's for you,' Sam said. 'You need a dressing over that cut on your eye to stop the bleeding.' Sam opened the case and let Luke rummage through it to select a dressing. 'Can you give me a couple of minutes before you move Ella? I need to get some pictures of the damage and I don't want them to see Trent. They've had enough trauma.'

'No.' Luke shook his head. Ella could barely speak. She was obviously in pain and her throat was probably sore as well. 'Ella can't wait. Can you move your car around the side of the big house, out of view?'

Sam nodded. 'Will you take photos of Ella's injuries? I'll need them for evidence.'

Luke photographed Ella's elbow and X-rayed her left arm. As expected, the X-ray showed a posterior dislocation of her elbow but there was no accompanying fracture which was good news. If there was such a thing as good news in this situation.

He explained the results of the X-ray, trying to

quell his feelings of guilt as spoke to Ella. If he focused on the medical facts he could put aside, for now, the idea that he'd let her down. That he should have stopped this somehow. Even if that was an unrealistic expectation to put on himself.

'I can put your elbow back into place but it will be sore,' he told her, unsure how much of what he was saying made sense. She was still sucking hard on the green whistle he'd given her for pain relief but he didn't take it away from her. She would need it when he relocated the elbow. 'I'm just going to get Penny to give me a hand with your elbow. I won't be long.'

He ducked out quickly, asking Penny to get Liv to sit with the receptionists and then come to assist him.

'Lie face-down on the bed, Ella, and let your arm hang over the side,' Luke instructed on his return as he lowered the back of the bed and helped her to lie down. 'Penny, I need you to hold Ella's left hand and apply gentle traction towards the floor.' Luke placed his thumbs on the back of Ella's elbow, gently applying a downward force to the olecranon process to realign the joint.

He fitted a sling for Ella and then got Penny to help as he photographed the bruising on Ella's neck. The bruising was in the shape of a man's hands, and Luke asked Penny to hold a tape measure against the finger marks so they could be compared for size against Trent's.

'Now, you need to let me attend to your eye,' Penny said as they completed the photos.

'I have to take a second X-ray and document Ella's injuries.'

'You can do that in a minute. Let Ella rest and come with me to my exam room.'

Luke was going to argue, to say that Penny could look at his eye just as easily in this room, but he could tell by her expression that she had things on her mind that she didn't want to say in earshot of anyone else. He sighed and got off the chair.

'I've asked Janine to reschedule the rest of the afternoon's list,' Penny said as she cleaned his wound, gluing the edges together. 'There was nothing urgent; she'll fit them in over the next couple of days.'

'I'm fine.'

'You're in no state to treat patients and someone needs to look after Ella.'

'I'm not doing a very good job of that,' he said as Penny's comment reminded him that he'd failed to protect her.

'It could have been worse, a lot worse, if you

hadn't got there when you did. This was her ex's doing. You're not to blame.'

Luke shook his head. He was unconvinced. 'What was I thinking, letting her stay in the barn? It wasn't nearly secure enough. Anyone could just drive onto the property, the door wasn't nearly as substantial as it looked and there was no escape exit.' In his mind, he had to accept some of the blame.

'You weren't to know that Trent would follow Ella halfway across the country,' Penny argued. 'Sam said Trent could have killed Ella if you hadn't been there. Sam will deal with him now. You need to take care of Ella. She's frightened and in pain. She needs to go home and lie down. And you look like you've gone two rounds in the boxing ring.'

'I'll look worse tomorrow,' Luke said, glancing in the mirror and touching his eyebrow. He knew the bruising would be worse in a day or two. 'Besides, Ella probably doesn't want me anywhere near her.' He wouldn't blame her if she never wanted to see him again.

'You saved her life,' Penny said in a tone that told him she thought he was being ridiculous.

But, while that might be true, he didn't expect any thanks. He had wanted her to stay in Pelican's Landing for selfish reasons and he'd

put her in harm's way. If he hadn't asked her to
stay, Trent wouldn't have been able to track her
down. How Trent had found her was a mystery
but Luke couldn't help feeling that it was somehow his fault.

Luke turned into his driveway and bypassed the
cottage, taking Ella and Liv directly to the big
house.

'Where are we going?' Ella asked as he missed
the fork in the driveway that led to the barn.

'I'm taking you to my place. I'm not leaving
you alone tonight.' As usual, Penny had been
right—Ella had been more than happy to let
him drive Liv and her back to the property—
but there was no way he was taking her back to
the barn.

'Penny said Sam will send Trent to Murray
Bridge, he'll be in custody overnight. We can
stay in the cottage.'

The effects of the analgesia from the green
whistle had worn off and he could see Ella's discomfort increasing. She needed some ice on her
elbow and some more pain relief.

'You can't manage Liv with one arm. You
need to let me take care of you tonight and I'm
not spending another night on your couch. It's

comfortable enough to sit on but it's not long enough to sleep on.'

He helped Ella out of the car and into the house, settling her on the couch. He gave her some pain relief and put an ice pack on her elbow. He put the television on for Liv, who was quite content lying on the floor watching cartoons with Maisie by her side.

'Do you need something for your head? Is it sore?' Ella asked him as she swallowed her tablets.

'No, it's fine.' His eye was swollen now, and he was having difficulty seeing out of it, but it seemed like a small price to pay compared to Ella's injury. 'I'll go and fetch some things for you from the cottage if you tell me what you need. I'll tidy up the mess and then make us all something to eat,' he said as his phone pinged with a message.

'That's Sam,' he continued as he read the text. 'He wants to come and take a statement from you, if you're up to it.'

The pain relief was making her drowsy and Ella had to concentrate hard as she listened to Sam speak.

'We've charged Trent with "assault occasioning bodily harm" based on what we witnessed but I need you to make a statement,' Sam told her.

'But I need to warn you, I expect he'll get released on bail tomorrow, if he can post it, but I'll ask for him to be sent back to Western Australia and for the bail conditions to prohibit him from leaving the state. He'll appear in court later, and if convicted he'll have a criminal record.'

'*If* convicted?'

'I can't see him escaping a conviction, but I will warn you that it's unlikely he will go to gaol if this is his first charge. And I couldn't find any previous convictions for him. I'm assuming he's got a prior history but, unless he's been charged before, there is no record. But we have served him with the intervention order, so if he breaches those conditions then gaol time would be a very real possibility. That should be enough of a deterrent to keep him away from you.'

'Do you know how he found Ella?' Luke asked when Sam had finished recording Ella's statement.

'He had a photograph from our local paper in his pocket. Apparently, someone Trent works with is related to the photographer, so he often looks at his photos. He'd met Ella before, when you worked at the marina in Geraldton, and he thought he recognised you in the picture so he showed Trent.'

Ella remembered the photographer who'd taken her picture on the day that Luke had rescued her and Liv from the flood. The one she'd turned away from, not wanting her photo taken.

'Trent turned up here on the chance Ella was still in Pelican's Landing. He figured you would have put Liv in school, so he waited outside the primary school and followed them home. We've got footage of his car on CCTV going past the school.'

Ella felt sick. All her planning and still he'd found her so easily.

'So it was my fault,' Luke said. He looked stricken with guilt.

'How is it your fault?' she asked.

'I asked you to stay in Pelican's Landing. If you'd moved on when you wanted to, Trent wouldn't have found you.'

'This isn't your fault. This is all on Trent.' She hated the idea that he would blame himself. 'You saved my life, Luke,' she said, knowing that was a debt she could never repay.

Ella slept fitfully in the same room as Liv. Despite knowing that Trent was spending at least one night in custody, she hadn't wanted to let Liv out of her sight. It was for Ella's peace of mind, rather than any real threat.

Luke had moved an arm chair into the room, as Ella found it more comfortable to be in a semi-reclined position, but despite this, and plenty of pain relief, her arm kept her awake for most of the night. Luke gave her more analgesia in the early hours of the morning and she finally fell into a deep sleep not long before sunrise.

She woke to the sound of cockatoos. She was briefly disoriented and, when she saw Liv's empty bed, she panicked for a moment until she saw Luke's note propped on Liv's pillow.

We're downstairs having breakfast. Kettle is on when you wake up.

Luke and Liv were in the kitchen. Liv was sitting at the table with a bowl of cereal and Luke was making a sandwich. He was packing Liv's lunch box and Ella realised he and Liv must have been across to the cottage while she slept.

'Good morning,' he greeted her as she kissed the top of Liv's head. 'How are you feeling?'

'Like a punching bag.'

'I'll drop Liv at school,' Luke said. 'You stay here and rest.'

But Ella shook her head. She didn't want to stay in the house alone but, more than that, she had things she needed to do. 'Would you be able to drop me in town?' she asked. She knew she wouldn't be able to drive today, her arm was too sore but she was hoping that tomorrow would be a different story.

'I can get whatever you need at lunch time.'

'I need some bags to start packing.'

Luke's brow furrowed. 'Packing?'

She'd decided, during her restless and sleepless night, that she and Liv would have to leave Pelican's Landing, and since the flood she'd accumulated enough things that meant she would need a few bags to pack it all up in.

Liv had finished her breakfast and was sitting quietly, listening intently and obviously hoping Ella wouldn't notice. 'Liv, can you go and get dressed and clean your teeth, please?' Ella asked, wanting to get her out of the room. 'Now, please,' she added, as she could see Liv about to argue.

'We can't stay here,' Ella told Luke once Liv had headed upstairs.

'With me?'

'In Pelican's Landing,' she clarified. 'I'd hoped we could be safe here but Trent has found us once. He knows where we are. What if he comes back?' She appreciated Luke's help but she was also upset that she needed it. Upset and angry that Trent's actions had put her in this position. She knew Luke would say he didn't mind helping but she was sure one day he'd get tired of coming to her rescue. She had brought Trent into her life and now into Luke's. If she'd stuck to her plan of moving to Queensland instead of being seduced by a kind man and good sex, she wouldn't have been in this position. Trent wouldn't have found her.

'You heard what Sam said last night,' Luke replied. 'Trent will be charged with assault and sent back to Western Australia. The interim intervention order has also been served—he can't afford to come near you again.'

The decision to leave was tearing her in two. She desperately wanted to stay in Pelican's Landing but she was terrified. It felt like a huge risk, but she was worried the price of staying would be too much to pay. She was worried it could cost a life—hers, Liv's or Luke's.

Luke had saved her life once and the only way to repay the debt was to make sure Trent couldn't hurt any of them ever again.

'Do you really think he'll pay attention to a piece of paper telling him to stay away from us?'

She wasn't convinced. She'd heard too many stories of people, mostly women, being subject to continued harassment and violence by their partners despite legal restrictions. She'd expected, hoped, that Luke would say that everything was under control, so she was surprised when he shook his head and agreed with her.

'I hate the fact you feel you have to leave but I understand that you can't afford to take the chance. I'm sorry I let you down,' he said.

Ella shook her head and reached out for him with her good arm. 'You didn't,' she hastened to reassure him, hating that Trent's actions had forced her into this position. 'This is on Trent, not you. If you hadn't arrived when you did, I wouldn't be here now. He would have killed me. I can't afford to take that chance again; I have to do what's best for Liv. Our safety has to be my priority.'

Ella had called a taxi to bring her home from town with the bags she'd bought for packing. She packed their things, stripped the bed and put a load of washing into the machine, hanging the sheets on the line with difficulty as she only had one good arm, before tackling the cleaning. Luke had moved the broken table and cleaned up the smashed crockery and she wondered when he had done that. It must have been last night. It was one less thing for her to worry about, but the whole cleaning-up process took far longer than it should have because of her aching elbow. But she had to keep going.

Sam had arranged for someone to collect Trent's hire car, which had been left parked in front of the cottage, blocking her car into the driveway. Once her car was clear, she was able to fetch Liv from school. She brought her home and then began to load their things into the car. She was planning to leave today. She was in fight or flight mode and she knew if she delayed it would only make it harder to leave. She needed to get going before she lost her resolve.

But she hadn't counted on histrionics from Liv. She was inconsolable, having just been told they were leaving Pelican's Landing, her school, her new friends, Luke and Maisie, and Ella was finding it difficult to offer any comfort given that she was exhausted, in pain and also reluctant to leave. But not wanting to go was very different from having to go.

She had just packed the last bag and was trying to convince Liv to get in the car when Luke and Penny arrived at the cottage. She had hoped to be on the road before Luke came home from work. She didn't know if she was strong enough for a face-to-face goodbye but all of a sudden that was the situation they found themselves in.

Penny took Liv outside to say goodbye to Maisie, leaving Ella and Luke alone.

'Are you sure you want to go?'

She didn't want to leave but she was scared. Scared to stay. Scared of Trent. Scared to rely on Luke. 'I want to be brave,' she said, 'but I need to be safe. I was lucky you arrived when you did yesterday, but you won't always be there, and I have to put Liv first. If something happens to me, Liv has no one. I've made plenty of mistakes in my twenty-six years and I'm trying not to make any more. This is what I have to do.'

She kissed him for the last time. Her heart ached as he held her tight but eventually he had to let her go.

'Goodbye, Luke.' She hurried outside, needing to put some distance between them before she changed her mind.

'Will you let me know when you get to Mildura?' he asked as he followed her to the car.

Ella nodded before bending down to strap Liv into her seat. She fought back tears as she drove away, leaving Luke and Penny standing in front of the barn. She couldn't let Luke see her cry. She knew her resolve would wash away if she started crying now.

She managed to hold it together until she hit the outskirts of town, before she had to pull over to give in to her distress. She and Liv cried until their tears ran dry. Liv fell asleep but Ella needed to keep driving. She looked in the mirror at Liv, to remind herself of the reason she was leaving, and started the engine again. This time she drove away without looking back, hoping her heart would recover.

With time and distance, she was certain it would.

'You couldn't convince her to stay?' Penny asked Luke as they watched Ella drive away.

Luke shook his head. 'She's convinced this is the only way. I can't tell her what to do. She wants to be in control of her own life. That's her right.'

'That didn't mean she had to leave.'

'I know that but she didn't feel safe. I couldn't protect her. Not always. She was right not to rely on me.'

But Ella's departure had left him feeling broken. He hadn't been looking for a relationship, but he'd found one. He'd offered her the cottage, thinking he was making a small sacrifice that would make a big difference to Ella, but he hadn't counted on the difference she was going to make to his life.

But he'd let her down and she was right to leave.

But, if that was true, he couldn't explain why it felt so wrong.

'Ella doesn't need someone to rely on in a physical sense,' Penny said, clearly not finished giving her opinion. 'She's been on her own on and off for years. What she needs is someone to love her.'

Ella's tears had subsided but the events of the past two days had left her exhausted. She drove into Loxton, a mere two hours from Pelican's Landing, and decided she couldn't keep driving, not today. She had wanted to get to Mildura but this would have to do. Her elbow ached and she was too fatigued and upset to drive any further.

Every mile further away from Pelican's Landing and Luke she'd driven, she'd felt more bereft, as if she was leaving a little trail of herself behind. She imagined little pieces of her broken heart littering the highway behind her and she knew she'd made a mistake. She was still letting Trent and his actions dictate how she lived her life.

She checked into a caravan park, grateful that the school holidays were over and there was a vacancy, and called Luke.

'Ella? Are you in Mildura already?'

Luke's voice calmed her mind but how she wished he was there beside her. How she wished she could step into his arms.

'No. I stopped at the caravan park in Loxton.'

'Are you okay?'

'No. Not really.' She was emotionally and physically exhausted. 'My elbow is aching; I probably shouldn't have driven and I think I've made a mistake.'

'You need to rest. Don't push yourself. You've had a tough few days.'

'I'm not talking about driving. I'm talking about Trent.'

'I don't understand.'

'I've let Trent control me. I wanted to be brave and I wanted to be safe but I've let him win. By leaving you, I've let him win. I don't want that.'

'Oh, Ella, you're not the only one who's made a mistake. I let you down and I'm sorry.'

'You haven't let me down. None of this is your fault.'

'I thought you would be better off without me. I thought you were better off sticking with your plan of building a future for you and Liv by yourself.'

'I thought that was what I had to do but I'm not so sure now. I miss you.' She hadn't intended to tell him that but her brain was too tired to think one step ahead.

'I miss you too,' Luke said before he went quiet.

Ella checked her phone, thinking she had lost reception, but the call was still connected. 'Luke? Are you still there?'

'Yes. I was just thinking.'

'About…?'

'Do you trust me?'

'Yes.'

'Okay. Stay where you are. Don't check out tomorrow. Don't do anything until I speak to you again.'

'What are you going to do?' she asked.

'What I should have done earlier. Get some sleep and don't go anywhere. I promise, everything is going to be all right.'

'Luke! Luke!' Liv flew off the jumping pillow and ran at full speed towards the gate in the playground fence as Ella turned around, her brow creasing in confusion as she saw Luke walking towards them.

'Luke!' She stood up from the bench where she'd been sitting watching Liv and went to meet him. 'What are you doing here?'

'I was worried about you.'

'I'm okay,' she said, her reply automatic, the fib rolling of her tongue. She'd become so accustomed to the lie.

'Are you really?' he asked and Ella shook her head.

Luke opened his arms and she stepped into his embrace. Her elbow protested as he hugged her to him but she didn't care. All she cared about was that he was there. 'I'm glad you're here,' she admitted. 'But I don't understand.'

'You've been brave. I needed to be as well,' he said as he released her,

'What are you talking about?'

'I wanted you to stay with me in Pelican's Landing but I thought you would be better off without me. I let Gemma and Mikayla down; I didn't want to let you down too. I should have asked you to stay, but I was scared, and I also didn't want you to think I was trying to control you. You are in charge of decisions about your life. And Liv's. But the past twenty-four hours have been the longest and loneliest of my life, and when you said you missed me I thought I had one last chance to fix things. I came to see if I can convince you to change your mind.'

'About?'

'Moving to Queensland. If you don't want Trent to win, would you consider coming back to Pelican's Landing with me? I love you, Ella, and, while I can't promise never to let you down, I can promise to try my best not to.'

'Can you say that again?'

'I promise to do my best not to let you down.'

'Not that bit, the other part.'

Luke smiled and repeated, 'I love you.'

Ella's heart leapt with delight. 'I love you too.'

He took her hands in his. 'Come back to Pelican's Landing with me,' he said. 'Make your home there with me, surrounded by people who love you. We're not going to let Trent win. Please, come back with me. Start over with me. Let's make a new life together.'

'You're not getting tired of rescuing me?'

'I'm not here to rescue you, I'm here to ask you to come home with me.'

'Home,' Ella repeated. 'I like the sound of that.'

'Is that a yes?'

She nodded and Luke smiled and picked Liv up, sitting her on his hip. 'Pack your things, Liv, we're going home!'

Liv clapped her little hands as Luke wrapped his free arm around Ella, drew her to his side and said, 'Kiss me like you've missed me…and then let's go home.'

EPILOGUE

'ARE THE GIRLS ASLEEP?' Luke asked as Ella stepped out onto the veranda of the big house.

'No.' Ella smiled and kissed Luke's cheek before she sat on the outdoor couch beside him. 'But they are in bed, trying to decide what their favourite bit of the day was.'

'What's the answer so far?'

'I think the tube rides are winning.'

It was Liv's sixth birthday and she had spent the day on the river with three friends from school. Luke had spent most of the day towing them behind his boat on an inflatable tube before they'd had a barbecue and a bonfire with marshmallows. The girls were all staying for a sleepover and Ella was preparing herself for a late night. But she wouldn't have changed a thing. It had been a perfect day.

When Ella had decided to return to Pelican's Landing with Luke, she and Liv had moved permanently into the big house, and it was the best decision Ella had made. The past eleven months had been eventful but only in a good way. Ella and Liv were safe and happy and loved.

She nestled in against Luke's side, tucking her feet underneath her and resting her head on his chest. The moon was rising behind the cliffs and she watched in awe as the golden sphere made its way into the sky. The view on the river was constantly changing. No two days were the same: misty mornings and golden sunsets; calm water and howling wind that bowed the willow trees; thunderstorms and cloudless days; pink, blue and orange skies. But she never tired of it.

'I forgot to tell you in all the birthday excitement that I got another bookkeeping client yesterday—the newsagent. Can you believe it?' Since completing her bookkeeper's training, Ella had managed to secure several clients in town and had also had a couple of referrals to businesses in neighbouring towns as well. She was earning her own money instead of relying on government hand-outs. She was supporting Liv and herself and was contributing to the household expenses as well. She was also volunteering at a women's shelter in the next town, assisting with financial advice, and the cottage, with its improved security, was now being regularly used for women in need of temporary accommodation to escape domestic violence.

'I can believe it. Your reputation is growing and I'm not surprised at all. I'm really proud of what you've achieved.'

'Thank you,' she replied. She was proud of how far she had come in a relatively short time. Her world had become big and exciting. 'But I couldn't have done it without your support.' Luke had been amazing. Just knowing he believed in her and had her back had been enough for her to challenge herself and she'd met every challenge so far.

She shifted on her seat, trying to get comfortable, as she was reminded that another challenge was coming their way, and that she'd better make the most of any peaceful moments she might be lucky enough to have in the next few months, as her peace and quiet would be coming to an end soon—even if only temporarily.

'Are you okay?' Luke asked.

'I'm fine but the baby's restless; he's kicking me in the ribs.' Ella took Luke's hand and placed it on her belly. She was almost six months' pregnant. She felt enormous but knew she was barely showing. It had been another hot summer so she was feeling slow and laborious; tired.

'He?'

'I'm positive we're having a boy. This pregnancy is so different from Liv's. Liv was quiet in the womb.' This pregnancy was different in so many ways. Both physically and mentally. She was safe, secure. Confident in her ability to raise a child. This time with a man she loved by her side.

Luke rubbed her stomach. 'Hello, Max, this is your dad.'

'Max?' Ella queried. 'You have a name for him?'

Luke nodded. 'Max—short for Maximus. It means "strong". I have no doubt our son will be strong of character. He'll get that from you.'

'What if I'm wrong and it's a girl?'

'I have a name for her too—it's Mildred. It means "gentle strength".'

'I'm not sold on Mildred.'

'How about Millie for short?'

'I like that,' she said as Luke's phone rang.

He took it out of his pocket. 'It's Christine.'

Christine was the new doctor who was due to start work at the clinic in a week's time. Ella hoped she was ringing to confirm some arrangements, not ringing with bad news. Christine and her husband were looking for a tree change. Christine was in her early fifties, not nearing retirement age yet, but her husband hadn't been well, and Christine had decided they needed a change of scenery and a slower pace and better work-life balance. She didn't want to spend sixty hours a week at work, she wanted time with her husband.

It had been Ella's suggestion for Luke to look for someone like Christine, and Ella hoped that having someone experienced on board would give Luke time to spend with their expanding family and with his father, whose health continued to decline.

Luke finished the call and Ella relaxed. She'd been able to hear from Luke's side of the conversation that Christine was just calling with some questions; she wasn't reneging on the contract. She lifted her feet and exercised her ankles, circling her feet, which had a tendency to swell at the end of a hot day.

'I'll just make you a cup of tea and then I'll massage your feet for you,' Luke offered.

'That sounds like heaven,' she replied.

Ella closed her eyes and rested her head back on the cushion, her hands clasped across her stomach, feeling the baby turning somersaults inside her. She opened her eyes when she heard the screen door bang shut, signalling Luke's return.

'Happy birthday,' he said as he put her tea on

the coffee table, before handing her a white envelope he held in one hand and a gift-wrapped parcel which he had tucked under his arm. 'Another year older.'

'I'm happy to still be here to celebrate.' She still had occasional flashbacks to the assault but Sam and Luke had been right—Trent hadn't contacted her again and she was just beginning to believe that she and Liv might live happily ever after.

'And are you happy with me?'

'You know I am. I think you are the secret to my perfect life,' she said as she pulled him down to sit on the couch with her so she could kiss him.

'Open this one first,' Luke instructed as he handed her the envelope.

She slid her finger under the flap and pulled out a tube of sunscreen and some tourist brochures for Queensland.

'I thought we could spend a few days in Queensland once Christine has started work and settled in,' Luke said.

'You're going to take a holiday?'

Luke nodded. 'I'm hoping we can go before baby Max arrives.'

'And before I get too enormous,' she said. She knew Luke was enjoying her fuller figure but sometimes she felt so ungainly. She was normally so thin and the changes to her body were taking some getting used to. She didn't remember being uncomfortable or feeling huge when she'd been pregnant with Liv. But she really didn't remember much about that pregnancy at all.

'You're not enormous—'

'Not yet.'

'You are strong and healthy and you look beautiful,' Luke continued, ignoring her interruption. 'And I thought we could invite Hayley and Josh and their kids too. Liv will love the theme parks and the beach, but she'd enjoy Chloe and Jack's company as well. What do you think?'

'It sounds fabulous. As long as we stay somewhere with an amazing pool so I can float around like a whale.'

'Okay, one amazing pool coming up. Now, your next present.'

The second present was shoe-box sized but, as she removed the wrapping paper and lifted the lid, she revealed a single piece of paper on which a large black question mark was written.

She looked up at Luke. 'What is this?'

'This gift comes with a question,' he said. 'I have given my life to my family, my father, my job and now this town. They all take a little piece of me, like a leaky tap—slow and steady so that I don't notice that I'm being drained—but you, you replenish me. Being with you restores me. You feed my soul. And when I'm with you I see a future—not just an existence but a life. You have saved me from a life half-lived and I want us to be a family, a proper family. You, me, Liv and all the babies still to come. I would like to adopt Liv, to officially make her my daughter, if you think she'd like me to be her dad.'

'She would love it. I would too.' Ella didn't doubt that Luke loved Liv, or her. He was constantly telling them as much, but she was profoundly touched to know he wanted to make it official. 'Is that the question?' she asked.

'That's a question but it's not *the* question. I know we've talked about getting married and you've said you don't need it. Perhaps my failed attempt has dissuaded you. But—' Luke got off the couch and down on one knee as Ella smiled '—I love you, Ella. I love everything about you—your beauty, your compassion, your strength—and I promise to stand by your side for the rest of our lives in any way that you would like me too. But what I would really like is to be your husband. Will you marry me?'

Tears sprang unbidden to Ella's eyes. She

blamed the pregnancy hormones, which could make her cry at the most inopportune times. She brushed them aside, wanting to be able to see Luke clearly. She was nodding as she spoke.

'I thought I could stand on my own two feet. I thought I wanted to be independent, and I'm sure I could have done that and been happy, but I know I wouldn't be *this* happy. You are everything I could possibly want and I want to spend the rest of my life with you. This is my home. My happy place. My sanctuary. Right here, with you. I love you and I do want to be married to you, to make our family complete. The answer, to both your questions, is yes. Liv loves you and I love you. Let's get married.'

* * * * *

If you enjoyed this story, check out these other great reads from Emily Forbes

Ali and the Rebel Doc
Marriage Reunion in the ER
The Perfect Mother for His Son
A Gift to Change His Life

All available now!